I0645213

Visions of
the Mutant Rain Forest

Robert Frazier

Bruce Boston

Crystal Lake Publishing
www.CrystallakePub.com

Crystal Lake Publishing
www.CrystallakePub.com

Be sure to sign up for our newsletter and receive
two free eBooks: http://eepurl.com/xfuKP

OTHER TITLES BY...

Robert Frazier
Phantom Navigation
The Daily Chernobyl and Other Poems
Perception Barriers
Nantucket Slayrides (with Lucius Shepard)
Co-Orbital Moons
Invisible Machines (with Andrew Joron)

Bruce Boston
Brief Encounters with My Third Eye
Sacrificial Nights (with Alessandro Manzetti)
Resonance Dark and Light
Dark Roads
The Guardener's Tale
Stained Glass Rain

Crystal Lake Publishing
Eden Underground by Alessandro Manzetti
Tales from The Lake Vol.3, edited by Monique Snyman
Gutted: Beautiful Horror Stories, edited by Doug Murano
    and D. Alexander Ward
Tribulations by Richard Thomas
Devourer of Souls by Kevin Lucia
Wind Chill by Patrick Rutigliano
Eidolon Avenue: The First Feast by Jonathan Winn
Flowers in a Dumpster by Mark Allan Gunnells
The Dark at the End of the Tunnel by Taylor Grant

Check out other Crystal Lake Publishing books
for Tales from The Darkest Depths.

CONTENTS

FICTION

POETRY

GENESIS

CRUISING THROUGH BLUELAND

Robert Frazier

In the dry season of a feverish year, when the earth baked throughout the Brazilian Shield, Jeri Cristobel sensed a change of climate, and like any gold miner who lived on rations of fear and superstition, he assumed that with it would come personal tragedy.

It seemed impossible to shrug off the smell of impending rain and concentrate on shouldering his dirt bags out of the pit to the placer troughs on the rim above. He rested atop each box-like plot busy with Serra Pelada's workers. Taking extra care, he climbed the tall ladders that clung against the walls like vines from the Hanging Gardens of Babylon, and he made comparisons between the pride and sin and avarice of that biblical city and life at the mine, although Serra Pelada was devoid of details like vegetation or carved stone. Just dirt and men. It reminded Jeri of a movie scene in which army ants had stripped a vat of beet sugar. The key element was motion...the dirt was shoveled into sacks, which in turn shifted to men's backs, who themselves moved up and down the crudely lashed ladders like beads on an abacus rack. Since the plots were so small, with their digging levels uneven, miners in the deepest recesses needed to move their loads in elaborate patterns that altered each day. The walls resembled a map of writhing flesh. And all of it at dusk on Saturday, including the dust-laden air, turned an eerie blood-red as Jeri quit work for the week.

ᘒ

It was pitch dark when Skaff Rios found Jeri nursing a warm glass of rum in town at the Plaza of Lies. After introductions, they discussed the quick onset of the rainy season and speculated if it, indeed, were an omen. Then the man produced a letter with news of the sickness that gripped Jeri's brother. Jeri's apprehensions found an immediate focus. He made his decision to return home, and notified the administrators that he was abandoning his plot deep in the pit, which, as several friends had pointed out, would soon be submerged by torrential downpours. He packed what mattered to him in a single duffle and squeezed it and his long limbs into Skaff's CJ-7, a rusty antique punctured with as much air as the man's personality.

Skaff looked soft under his blue suit, with manicured nails and scented oil on his jet-black hair; the physical opposite of Jeri, who had turned gaunt and deeply-tanned in the mine pit, worry lines grooving his face. At first, Skaff drove in resolute silence, enduring two days of violent showers and roach hotels, before he grew talkative, almost brotherly in tone—about his adventures as a drug smuggler. The big scores and expensive whores. His investments. His bribes to Blueboy soldiers in San Juan de Caceres. Jeri considered Skaff useful for entering Caceres, now capitol of the restricted zone of war games called Blueland, so he feigned interest in such talk. In his head, though, another voice mourned for the close fraternal ties his true brothers had shared, ties that the Blueboys had shattered. This infused his replies with bitterness. By the time they passed into the new affluence of the Mato Grosso, Jeri felt weak as a man twice his age, yet he sensed that the grueling ride had less impact on him than the inescapable conclusion that people like Skaff preferred their lives to be fractioned to a single elemental value...like greed.

Had he done any better by leaving Caceres for the gold mines? He liked to think so, liked to think the support he'd paid for his brother Eric kept the scales in balance.

The wet weather cleared on the third evening of travel, yet strips of cloud sailed across the moon and divided its light into swatches of silver and lagoons of shadow that threatened to swallow the jeep, to offer as dark a resolution to the journey south as the one Jeri feared awaited him at its end. The jeep dropped axle-deep in a mud hole. Skaff swore, wrenching the wheel to avoid the deep center. Jeri's gut fluttered with nausea. Hurled against his door, gulping for air, he almost regretted his acceptance of Skaff's ride from the working hell in the mines to the living horrors of Blueland.

⑃

Eric Cristobel slept spread-eagled in an underground level of the Jiboa Hotel, pinioned to his bare mattress. Underwear soaked and sheets balled on the wooden floor beside him. Sweat beaded under his dark bangs. He flowed in and out of consciousness like a wave breaking then receding on a ghostly shore, and though he tried to raise himself up, his movements were sluggish, ineffective. He tried again and jerked upright, contracting his stomach to get his torso sitting straight.

Muscles refused to relax. He felt like shit.

He wanted to imagine something beautiful, someone uplifting. He wondered where his brother Jeri lived, what exotic lands he traveled to. But this didn't matter, not really.

It felt like he was still dreaming, and he did not believe he would ever awaken.

ᘓ

The road smoothed out along a recently logged ridge, and Jeri could see flashes fifty kilometers to the south. He shuddered as he pointed at the storm gathering there.

"That's *malo*," he yelled to Skaff over the whine of the engine. "A mean squall."

It looked to Jeri as if they had plunged into the barrel of an immense artillery piece, where the thunderheads, held to a horizontal axis by strange meteorological forces, formed a corkscrew spiral, and lightning danced through its dark eye like threads of current jumping inside a supercharged coil.

"Yeah. I bet it's close to the city," Skaff said.

Jeri grunted in reply. He stared at the blue forks of light and wondered how he could have left his brother there. Blueland, a place where weapons like these were tested.

A stiff wind gusted through the jeep. Skaff waved a fleshy fist at the storm and beat the dash to a tune that crackled on the radio. The samba was loud and plaintive, and it seemed to Jeri that it was the music that tossed

Skaff's greasy black curls and lashed them about his jowls and sunken eyes. Huge rain drops drummed on the windshield, leaked through from the roof. They rolled their windows up, and Jeri arranged his poncho around the neck of his shirt and under his chinos until it covered all but his face. As Skaff maneuvered on the rutted highway, the headlights stabbed high and low through the roadside homesteads and shadowy tunnels in the forest ahead like the brush strokes of a painter filling a dark canvas. Billowing clouds obscured a pewter grey moon. The discharges flashed brighter.

"It's the Blueboys," Jeri said after a few more kilometers. "Playing for the hell of it. I've seen them tie tornadoes in knots."

Skaff nodded, but Jeri knew that he was still intent on the radio and didn't see what Jeri saw when they looked into the tempest. Skaff concerned himself with the high life, with running drugs into Blueland. He hadn't been born there. Skaff's older brother hadn't been pancaked under a building when the Blueboys caused *heavy rain:* percipitant sheets made heavy with isotopes. And his younger brother wasn't trapped in Caceres now, confined to a sickbed. Jeri wondered what he would think of Eric, how Skaff would react to such a destitute soul.

"Fucking Blueboys." Jeri spat with vehemence. "Caceres was beautiful until they came."

Jeri imagined packets of Skaff's drugs strapped somewhere under the jeep, and this paranoia heightened his agitation, as if the coke radiated homing signals that could attract every Blueboy in the territory. He swallowed hard. When the jeep hit a series of deep potholes, he grasped the armrest until his knuckles whitened.

"Yeah, places like Caceres go sour." Skaff rolled his window down as the rain abated some, and he brushed the water off his suit coat. "Damn this mugginess. Makes your balls cook."

He turned to Jeri with a toothy grin, but Jeri refused to smile back. Just nodded and pulled at his new growth of beard.

"Yup," Skaff continued. "I'm hot, and I'm almost home to Carlita!" He grabbed his crotch and let out a sarcastic laugh that was drowned in a sudden riff of static from the radio.

As they exited a funnel of trees onto another open stretch of hilltop, the jeep spooked a menagerie of birds that flapped about the windshield and winked out of the headlights, their existence reduced to absolutes, either in bright blurs or blackened smudges. Jeri recognized none of the species. A pterodactyl-like flyer lifted above them; Skaff braked and came to a bone-jolting halt. Meters from the steaming grill of the jeep stood the biggest wolf Jeri had ever seen, an Amazonian maned wolf of incredible proportions. Two more wolves loped up beside the first and held their ground in the bright headlights, pawing the dirt. They stood taller than draft horses, with bat ears and madder-colored hair bristling in a collar of fire about their heads. Their slick bodies seemed bound in place, sinews rooted in the soil, and they inched forward, their long tapered noses to the ground, night-reflective eyes flashing golden as coins.

Skaff babbled and gunned the accelerator, but the engine cut out. In the pale half light from the dashboard, Jeri saw a blue arm as it snaked away from the steering column. He looked past Skaff's scared profile, glimpsed the face of a Blueboy in a combat suit and a visorless helmet molded like brain coral. The wolves vanished, holographic projections that melted to fog. The trooper held up Skaff's keys.

"Real glad ya stopped by," the Blueboy said. His voice sounded no louder than a whisper, yet its coarse English sonics made an incision in Jeri's brain, worming its way inside. "Leave yer lights on. We'll be needin' to see papers on yer business in the region."

Skaff reached for the wallet in his coat. Aware that the Blueboys might take undue liberties in their inspection if he remained passive inside, Jeri opened his door and stepped down to the mud road on wobbly legs.

"We live here," he said, but could say no more.

The trooper moved to the passenger side of the jeep with impossible speed, and held Jeri under the chin, pinned him against the hood. Jeri began to struggle yet thought better of his heroics when the Blueboy applied pressure. He slid his hand behind him, hoping to reach his own ID card, but the trooper interpreted this as a hostile move and lifted him off his feet, smacked his head hard against the windshield. Jeri felt a ridge of coarse, synthetic skin cut off his wind pipe.

"Stop it," Jeri gasped.

"Ya ain't in no position to tell me nothin'. Some rebel's been takin' shots at us. And we'd just as soon torch this junker. Watch ya boil like crawdaddies."

"Listen here!" Skaff said from inside the cab.

"Oh, I am. And I don't like what I hear. Ya took the wrong road tonight."

"Got trouble, Trigger?" The new voice spoke with a smoother North American accent. "If not, then ease up."

The trooper released him, and Jeri slipped off the hood to his knees in a puddle. He coughed and rubbed at his chaffed neck. His stomach spasmed and he tasted bile, imagining it to be an emotion he'd built up over the years from this kind of treatment.

"Who is this?" asked the voice.

Jeri said as he stood, "I wasn't allowed to show my..."

The soldier throttled him again. "Ya don't talk to General Berkey unless spoken to."

"Trigger, let him loose."

General Berkey stepped from the shadows behind Trigger and covered the distance to them in two power-augmented strides. She was dressed in light battle armor with an officer's pentagram insignia, and she smiled, revealing a mouthful of shark's teeth inlayed in gold settings. Her lapis exoskin failed to mask the delicate structure of her face. The features were striking, and a dragon tattoo twined from her bare scalp around one eye. She reached out her empty hand. Baffled, Jeri stared at the burn scars that trailed along the lengths of her graceful fingers. Plastic nails retracted under flexible exoskin cuticles and left their hollow points showing. Instead of a thumbnail, a tiny video screen held a view of Skaff's jeep from a camera above and beside them. She cleared her throat. Jeri understood then and handed her his wallet.

The Blueboy leader flashed him a quizzical look when she read his ID, then strode off punching numbers on a row of pinpoint keys below the screen on her thumb. She returned after ten minutes of consultation, her face changed, as if to say, "I know who you are, Mr. Cristobel."

○♂

Eric awoke from yet another nap. Eyes fixed on the wall beyond the end of his bed.

Wallpaper began to breathe, to melt, its patterns of hibiscus flowers fusing into a large reddish blotch about five feet off the floor. Something pushed through the center of the blotch, and the wall stretched out taut and rubbery on the knobby protrusion. At first it appeared smooth, without detail, but the more Eric stared at the knob, the more it resembled a fist with four parallel fingers meeting at a bony row of knuckles. And as his full attention centered on this, a blue hand punched through the red stain and groped for the end of the mattress.

Eric held his breath. Lungs cried for air.

A muscular blue arm followed, covered with turquoise blood, and it grasped at the ragged edges of its entry hole. Began to tear the hole bigger. A dark shoulder and a portion of ebony chest pushed further into Eric's room. Eric rolled from bed. Bolted out the door into the dim hallway.

Shadows along the baseboards pooled into phantasms that lashed at his feet. Eric ran for the stairs. A bright yellow missile flashed through the wall on his right and passed into the wall on his left without leaving a mark on either surface, yet he thought he smelled the acrid fumes of exhaust. Sirens whistled, seemed to originate inside his head. He pitched forward on the green shag runner before the stairs and landed hard, his head smacking against the padding on the fifth riser. He stared at the pebbled grain of the carpet just inches before his eyes. A window stretched and bubbled into the riser, a window that looked down on a swirling city of spires and slums. The window moved, as if Eric were seated in a hoverchop skimming over the skyscrapers, and when he dipped over low buildings, the familiar peeling white manse of the Jiboa Hotel ballooned below him on the street. Several Blueboys were breaking into the front lobby, weapons ready.

He could hear the grunted commands and the thud of heavy boots on the staircase.

His viewpoint trailed them through a hallway, glided over their heads. He searched frantically for a safe place to hide from the chaos and pain that would come. Entered a dark rectangle, lit by a feeble bulb above the upper jam. Plunged down several flights of stairs. Fell smack on a prostrate body, sinking into it, deep into the recesses of the brain.

"Hey, this looks like the one."

The voice deep and resonant; it surrounded Eric where he lay on the steps. Someone nudged him with a boot, then kicked him. He tumbled back in a heap at the foot of the stairs.

"He must have heard us rounding up people on the upper levels and knocked himself unconscious trying to get out."

"Get Dirk to run a retinal scan. We need positive ID."

More gruff voices. Thick hands grabbed Eric under the armpits and jerked him up until he stood, feeling exposed in briefs and a stained tee-shirt. He was spun around to face his tormentors. Men laughed as they shined a pencil beam in his eye. They had wide blue faces and mouths filled with wicked teeth and black gums. Another soldier arrived from upstairs.

"Hurry up with the scan," the new one said. "I've got to confirm the capture over the comm."

"Shee-it. Isn't this the same kid we picked up last week? What gives?"

"Popular boy. The General wants him out at Delta Base by dawn. They're reeling him in."

Men on each side of Eric boosted him onto the first step as if he were a feather. Pushed and prodded until he started the awkward climb to ground level. Progress was slow. Projections and drug mists left his body twitching.

"Should we sedate him?"

"Why bother? He's already gone."

CB

General Berkey returned with Jeri's ID.

"All in order, Jeraldo. They're dated but quite valid. I'm intrigued by your history." Berkey said this with a sensuous curl of her tongue along the ridges of her teeth. "My apologies for the men. They're upset over an earlier incident."

"So I gathered."

She called to Trigger, who stood at the back of the vehicle poking a tire iron into the wheel well for the spare tire. "What about the driver?"

Trigger closed the well, then zipped up Skaff's bags and crammed Jeri's duffle on top of them. They were soaked with mud.

"He checks out, sir."

"You two can go," the General said as the rain quickened, beading on her cheeks and dropping little jewels from the tip of her nose.

She handed Jeri his ID and his wallet, and with her touch traced a mild stinging shock on the back of his hand. It dissipated along his forearm and burned from the shoulder down his chest to warm his groin. He felt as if he'd swallowed a mug of grain alcohol. His immediate erection strained against the fabric of his pants. Acids flared in his gut. He felt soiled. She'd juiced him with an E-pheromone, a tailored and often addictive drug that imprinted its victim for future susceptibility, a sexually specific susceptibility. Jeri opened the jeep door and collapsed in his seat as Skaff eased his foot off the clutch. He could still feel the heat of her caress and her glistening pupils scanning him as if the topography of his soul winked on a computer screen, revealing his weakness for mysterious women.

Skaff sped up. Jeri let the door flap open, let the drizzle pepper his face with cold bullets.

"C-C-Christ, that was close," Skaff said loudly. "I've got a load of coca paste in that spare."

As if to place emphasis on Skaff's relief, a powerful wind sighed through the cracks in Skaff's door. Skaff's emotional tone was clear to Jeri, however. It wasn't worry that drained out of Skaff's system now, or the sarcasm he'd thrown earlier at Jeri about unpleasant circumstances in Caceres. It was raw fear. A wild look shined in the man's eyes each time lightning crackled and spit in the sky ahead of them. Indeed, Skaff was a newcomer to the ways of Blueboy troopers and their games, and they'd gotten to him. Jeri caught his swinging door and slammed it shut just as thunder boomed overhead. He huddled under his poncho again.

"It was closer than you think," he said as Skaff slowed. "I'm not sure why, but my papers got us through with a minimal search."

Skaff didn't ask for clarification; he chewed gum and concentrated on the road. Ruts and potholes overflowed. The spatter soaked Jeri's ankle boots through a missing plate in the floor of the cab, and when the downpour came, it fluttered the canvas roof and slapped the windshield in sidewinding sheets that tongued along the glass around the frantic wipers. Jeri's stomach grew queasy again, its juices frothing and tossing like the leafy branches overhanging the road. He curled against the wet seat and closed his eyes. The jeep moved like a frigate cutting between the crests of tall, black waves. When Jeri nodded off, the present seemed light years away, a slip of coast in the foggy distance, while the past loomed in his thoughts like a steep rocky island.

He was born Jeraldo Cristobel, one of three brothers orphaned without birthplace or date, a matter that pained him with self-doubt in his youth. The three were settled in St. Sambuca, a drafty, stone church with a small walled enclosure in the back, where a cottage lipped the private bathing pond of an aging Father Superior rumored to have a taste for young boys. When all three had reached schooling age, Eric—whose sensitive mind could perform small miracles—was raped by this man. So, at the urging of his eldest brother Jerico, he snuck off with them to a nearby river and called into their bucket a swarm of can-diru for the Father's pond. The sliver-sized fish were called "piss fish" by the swamp fisherman who had to squeeze themselves off while they bathed, that or face castration when the tiny devils lodged themselves in the urethra. The Father Superior fared no better, and the boys' revenge welded them into a tight-knit unit— protective of each other—as they found themselves back on the streets of Caceres. A young hotel owner named Mama Lavao took them in, and Jeri, at age nine, buried himself in a routine of hard work and solid food. Though he mistrusted Mama's charity at first, Jeri grew content as the years passed, his muscles grew hard, and his smolder-ing eyes attracted many local girls.

When Jeri turned fourteen, the elite soldiers of the WestHem armies occupied the surrounding countryside for a full winter, a season of rain and mock violence. Each year thereafter these Blueboys stayed longer, staging more elaborate battles and tests until the fateful event that remained branded in Jeri's memory on a grand scale. The Blueboys' heavy rain, meant to be used on a condemned slum, flattened an adjacent neighborhood, taking Jerico with it. Eric retreated to his own fantasia of grief and self-pity. Jeri escaped this fate by leaving Caceres at twenty for Sao Paolo. Within a few years, though, his fortune was stitched in aimless patterns across the Brazilian outback. Now, he was giving up that freedom.

By the time they reached the far edge of the *Planalto do Mato Grosso*, Jeri felt better though still feverish from the drug. He sat up and watched the sunlight leak over the hills and dust the foliage a faint silver. The jungle developed like a photographic plate; first the imperceptible brightening, then a breakdown of solid shadow into visible forms, then the grainy details. The rising sun torched the fine spider-webbing of cracks in their windshield and turned the vegetation they passed to a molten riot of yellows and parrot greens. At last, it cleared the horizon.

Complaining of stiffness and exhaustion, Skaff pulled over onto a wide shoulder where the road snaked off the heights to the city, which hugged the foot of the hillside and the very edge of the valley below. They sat, hypnotized by the Pantanal where it stretched southeast in the distance like a glittering plain of light, pocked with islands and great weedy domains. Only the Gran Chaco stood wholly aloof from the floodwaters. It ran to the west, a low, sparsely-wooded climax forest that swallowed eastern Bolivia and half of Paraguay.

"See, it's beautiful country," Skaff said to Jeri.

"Sure, but it doesn't resemble anyplace that WestHem would defend against EastHem. The soldiers don't belong here for training."

"They have to train somewhere."

"In the North American cities, if they must. But invasion there seems just as unlikely. The West has conceded Europe and Africa for Latin America and the Pacific Islands. The world's split fairly."

"Doesn't matter," Skaff said. "Armies are armies."

After they watched a pair of rudderless, cigar-shaped gunships—termed "hoverchops" by the Blueboys—glide silently past them and dip over the checkerboard of Caceres below, Jeri lit a cigarette and began to talk again, not willing to let the subject drop.

"Want to hear something weird?" he said.

"Yeah." Skaff popped a second stick of gum into his cheek.

"My friend, The Impresario, said in the letter you delivered that Eric had a theory. Something about a mass psychological experiment being used on the city this year. Funny, eh?"

Skaff said, "Like we're mice in a maze."

Jeri coughed and flicked his ashes out the vent window. Then he rolled his main window down for air.

"More like lab rats."

"I didn't know your brother was an intellectual."

"He isn't. That's his delirium. But it could be true. He has a knack for knowing things. I've seen him guess names. Seen him call fish and caimans up from the swamp waters."

Skaff snorted in disbelief.

Jeri knew, though. He and his brothers had been monitored in their teens by Blueboy scientists, and Eric, at least, possessed a talent, an eerie potential they wanted to groom. Also, Jeri knew firsthand about the neural disruptions: the drug mists, subliminal fear waves and the projected images the soldiers used. The disruptions had dredged strange things from his soul, until he couldn't stand it. He had to flee. But Eric had stuck it out. Suddenly the guilt swelled in Jeri's heart. The same old guilt. He'd escaped, but left Eric to fend for himself.

Jeri grew anxious to see his brother. He stubbed his cigarette on his boot heel and dropped the half-finished butt through the gap in the jeep's floorboard. He wondered if Skaff had ever jettisoned contraband through the hole.

"Let's get going," he said.

Skaff turned the ignition over. They bounced onto the road and slipped down the windy bends to the city and the immense swamplands that bordered it. The descent was bracing. On the last curve that straightened out into the wide basin they skirted the Caceres airbase with its small spacepad that served a fledgling colony on Mars. Here—it had been rumored—Jeri's father Paulo had emigrated after deserting their mother to the Chagas fever.

"Road check," announced Skaff.

Several Blueboys in black and tan camouflage suits stood at attention by their guard booths. One motioned them to stop. Skaff handed over their IDs with an envelope of money. The guard consulted his computer.

"You've already been scanned," he said. He returned the cards and waved them on.

They drove through the outer barrios of Caceres, and into a fog of psychomist blown off course from a Blueboy exercise further into the swamps. This tripped an emotional release which sent Skaff into paroxysms of laughter about the money he'd wasted on the guard, but it left Jeri sick with his head out the window. He let it all out, as if it were physical evidence of the frustrations that had stewed in him during the trip home, and he made a promise to himself to get Eric out of Blueland at any cost.

∛

Outside Eric's cell window a raucous company of white, nearly transparent macaws twisted in the air and dipped, much the way fish schooling in the river currents flitted this way and that by the workings of some genetic, communal instinct. Eric imagined that he'd been transported underwater, to the forests that flooded along the tributaries during the rainy season, and now that mystical place held him in stasis between land and water, earth and fire, between all elements that bound the universe. He remembered the incident with the candiru. Remembered how his brothers instinctually thought as one in the old days, and he felt sad. He wanted his family again. Wanted simple days glowing with their camaraderie.

In a ceiba tree that arched over the cell, a monkey nibbled on epiphytes, and it looked to Eric like a smudge or a shadow. Spirit creature; all soul, no substance. He called for the beast to come closer, for he wanted to see its fur up close, to marvel at what brilliant stroke of adaptive camouflage it possessed. It remained elusive in front of him, though, with no individual details ever coming into focus. He could use that. With such protection, he could fool the blue men that would come to deliver him to the court of the Blue Queen. The woman who'd summoned him before. Forced him into tests. Forced him to tell her everything and anything she wanted. And in the end, she'd plied him with stimulants and kept him awake through the night with the heat of her touch. Forced him to love her. Hate her. Be dependent on her.

The door rattled, and the one named Trigger opened it and pulled Eric to his feet. Stepping outside, Eric blocked the mid-morning sunlight with his hand and slumped against the outside wall of his cell.

"Ten minutes," the Blueboy said.

Eric nodded. Sun felt wonderful on his skin.

Giving up on any effort to steady himself, he slid his back down the bumpy fiberglass wall and sat with his legs straight out in front of him. He basked with his face turned toward the sun. His lizard brain, the tiny bulb of instincts that ruled his body, hummed beneath the more developed lobes of his cerebrum. He tuned out the psychobabble that ran through his head about his life at the Jiboa Hotel, about his friends, about his role as guinea pig for the Blueboy scientists. Though he sensed none of the prescient visions that had confused him before the kidnapping, his thoughts still weren't clear. Pervasive dread ghosted through him. A confrontation awaited.

He shut it out. Tried not to think of it, or to see beyond to its resolution. Just vegetated in the sun.

"Ten minutes are up," the Blueboy said. "Time to show the General what yer hidin' from us."

Eric tried to raise himself, but he felt weak. The Blueboy helped him up. He had not expected this, yet he was grateful. He wiped his dirt-specked palms on the khaki pants they'd issued him, looked around at the compound he must cross.

It was a small rent in the canopy of trees along the edge of the Pantanal, and it contained three glass and white concrete research buildings, a long row of quonset huts, a small landing field with one hoverchop, and a pair of confinement cells including his own. Since he'd last been there, they'd poured a pad for the hoverchop and now a crew of Blueboys cleaned up the brush piles about the buildings. Yet the atmosphere remained the same. The base looked temporary. Five years in the future the main buildings would be reduced to concrete bunkers, and the rest would be stripped from the soggy land. Twenty years from now the swamp would silt over the location, mangroves taking hold with steely roots.

"Move it."

The Blueboy gripped Eric by the arm and tugged him toward the largest building in the compound. The walk seemed to take forever.

Inside an anteroom lit by skylights and tall narrow windows with screens, three Blueboys conversed. One, the Blueboy scientist who would ask Eric questions and record the answers with rows and rows of dials. One, the medical technician who would administer drugs. One, the Blue Queen.

The Blue Queen approached him while the others continued a conversation consisting of technical jargon. She dismissed Trigger with a nod.

"Eric! I haven't seen you for a week." She held his hand and stroked it as if it were a purring cat. "I'm glad you agreed to return."

"Agreed?" he said, though his throat constricted.

"Why, yes." She pressed her fingers into his arm until they dug tiny curves into his muscles. "At least I hope you plan to stay."

Eric felt a prickly heat that expanded within. Could say nothing. Thoughts became random and burned out of control.

A church parade had gathered a small crowd along the avenue, and a commotion started outside the lobby of the Jiboa Hotel as Jeri and Skaff parked the jeep. A Blueboy on solo patrol lifted two teenagers by the backs of their necks and let out a scream that forced Jeri to cover his ears. The kids, who copied the dress and skin color of Blueboys as part of a youthful fad, twitched and jerked. The soldier left the kids collapsed on the pavement, blood leaking from their ears. Jeri pulled them inside while Skaff called an ambulance. After the vehicle arrived, and they'd given brief statements that Jeri knew would be ignored by local officials, he led Skaff to the core of the building, where stairways started down and a great elevator well showcased an antique machine.

Other than the tiny lobby, this comprised the only part of Jiboa used above ground. The rest had been abandoned when Mama Lavao moved the hotel rooms underground in fear of another heavy-water rain shower, or equivalent horrors not yet unleashed by the Blueboy scientists. And business had boomed for a hotel in a state with restricted travel. Customers preferred the structure's womb-like safety, and claimed that the neural disruptions conjured by the war games were eliminated below ground. Negated for all except Eric. Eric sensed even the most distant weapons employed for effect, and so the brothers' rooms were housed at the bottom-most level, where at least the effects on him were diminished.

"We must go down," said Jeri as he pointed to a set of stairs. He was still upset by the incident on the street.

Skaff shook his head. "I've never taken the elevator. Let's ride."

The ironwork cage had been replaced by a clear seamless bubble, but the elevator ran on the original system of gears and cable-car lines. Its slow descent along a helical track was impressive. Jeri, however, remembered the stairs down to the four subterranean levels, the twisting and turning cases that were colored in whatever exotic paints Mama could find. These felt like the soul of the hotel to him, and they gave rise to the hotel's present name. The multi-hued Jiboa snake slinked along the edges of the Pantanal, staying within its camouflage of vegetation.

"But the stairs are quicker."

"I've been driving three days, a few minutes more won't matter."

Jeri nodded, and as they boarded the elevator, a heavyset woman with a singular grace to her form and movements squeezed in with them. She clasped Jeri to her broad breasts, with no care as to the sensuality of the gesture, and she held his head between them. He straightened up. Her wide bronze face, without lines save for the perfection of the curves about her soft mouth, smiled beneath a profusion of red-brown curls scented with orchids. She wore a floral dress and a gold crucifix.

"Jeraldo," Mama Lavao said, as if the one word explained a longing hidden in the regal planet of her body. She punched a button and the three of them began to drop along the track. "I arrived too late to help with the ambulance, but I'm so happy to see you." Her smile collapsed. "Eric is gone, though."

Jeri turned rigid and looked Mama in the eye. "Gone? When?"

"The bad boys came late last night. They've come before, but never like this. They just busted through the building."

"Why Eric? Do they still test him?"

"Yes."

"The Impresario didn't say *that* was the problem with his health."

"We avoided the truth in our letter, just to allow Mr. Rios to get it past inspection. I'm sorry. I always managed to get him healthy again with the money you'd send. And I didn't think they were testing diseases on him, or anything. Just wearing him down." Her hazel eyes glazed with remorse. "He never quite recovered inside, though. He'd see them coming for him before it happened. Or have visions of mutated beasts from the swamp. Crazy things, you know."

Skaff cleared his throat. "Drugged. He's drugged."

"I suppose," she said as tears ran along her cheeks. "Only there was little sign of it in his body. They worked on his head. The bad boys want his gift, you know."

The elevator passed the landing for the second sublevel, and Jeri shook with rage. He stared up at the track that spiraled above them, and tried to divine a message in its twists, a revelatory pattern in the chaos of the world. They had Eric. He'd come home to repair the past; now Eric appeared beyond reparation.

"Where did they take him?"

"We don't ask. I can't afford to. The less I ask questions, the better it is for everyone at the hotel."

"Who would know, Mama?"

"The Impresario, if anyone," said Skaff.

"Possibly," Mama added, brightening again. "He'd talk with Eric quite often."

Jeri remembered the diminutive man who resided at Jiboa, the survivor of a wargames accident that left him without an organic lower body. Several of Mama's staff were scarred by the military games, for she made a point of helping out that way, but The Impresario was her sole charity case as a boarder...save Eric, when he could no longer work. The Impresario holed up in the hotel, voicing a grudge against those who ruined him. But he accepted his fate. Jeri no longer felt capable of that.

The elevator docked at the third level of Jiboa with a jolt, and the door slid open. Mama stepped out and waited for Jeri and Skaff.

"The Impresario's in the Commons, Jeri. I'll see you for dinner?"

"Both of us are starved, if that's okay? Skaff's had a long drive."

"He's welcome."

Jeri watched Mama stop at the mouth of a hallway, turn back and try to smile. She limped away.

"I don't think she likes me," Skaff commented.

"She's distracted."

Jeri heard the Impresario's sing-song voice echo from another hall, so they followed the sound. They found him on the burgundy rug of the Commons, holding court for a group of Americans with their video cameras.

In his mid-sixties, The Impresario reached medium height when he bobbed high on his bionic legs—crab legs—of fitted brass and fiber optic circuits lit in orange and yellow. He held his back ramrod straight, though with a certain social poise that affected a relaxed and imperious attitude one might expect of a man trained within a strict Argentinean military school. He was robust once, at the time Jeri had left for the mines, but a slow deterioration now gripped him, perhaps one of the unnamed diseases of a metamorphosing Amazonia. His neck showed all its veins and sinews. The cuffs and collar on his blue uniform seemed baggy about his bony hands and shriveled neck. He still managed to keep his bald head shined, his white goatee trimmed, and his orator's voice, obviously, in good timbre.

"Ladies and gentlemen, I've been ghostin' more and more of late." His face glowed with the light of rapture. "I've seen the hours raise their dark rigging. They're sailing away. Sailing toward that future moment, that skirmish with the powers that be. I can feel it up there, up the line."

"Tell us more," Jeri called out. The Impresario swiveled at the hip, broke into a laugh. He shouted louder, drawing the walls in closer with his gestures.

"This man's seen it too. We've got to react now. Get out in the streets and raise our throats to the wind."

"Amen," Skaff said, surprising Jeri.

"Yes, friends. We'll let the bells toll in our jaws. Let our voices climb. Or else we'll be digging graves again with our fingernails and feeling our bones ripen in the great heat. Things are coming to a head. Just you wait and see!"

The group tittered, clacking away in English.

Skaff took a deep breath. "Either we move with it, or we get swallowed in the dust."

The political vein of their talk intrigued Jeri. He considered the possibility that Skaff and The Impresario were kindred souls. They spoke as if using a code of chivalry, masking their displeasure with WestHem in rococo phrases.

"Friends," The Impresario said with the slightest dip to effect a bow. "If you'll excuse me. I've business to talk with these fine gentlemen."

The group bowed in return, and wandered off toward the hallway with nervous expressions on their faces. The Impresario strutted closer with some measure of skill on his mechanical limbs.

"Ah, Jeri. I've been expecting you." The man canted as far forward as his frame allowed, and gave Jeri a firm hug. The old man sighed. Then he broke away and swiveled to greet Skaff.

"Pleased to see you, good man." The Impresario shook Skaff's hand with vigor. "Most people call me The Impresario."

"I know. I'm Skaff Rios. I delivered your letter." Skaff brushed a hand through his hair. "Tell me, who were they?"

"A scientific group that's studying the swamp. But I believe it is a cover for an eccentric man, the tall black one weighted with gold necklaces."

"How eccentric?"

"Mama says he is a gourmet cook of exotic foods. And he understands the Blueboys are mutating plants and animals in the swamp. I think he's interested in collecting specimens for his greenhouses as well as his studies."

Jeri groaned. "I just lost my appetite."

The Impresario spun at the waist and returned his attention to Jeri.

"I've missed you."

"It was your note that brought me."

"Our Eric has been taken. You've heard, haven't you?"

"From Mama, yes. And I know why."

"Oh?" That captured the interest of both men.

"We had a run-in at the border. Blueboys looking for guerrillas. They ran a check on me and no doubt realized that they'd better scoop Eric up while they could still find him. It was that damn Berkey woman."

A twinkle caught fire in The Impresario's brown eyes, and he seemed to give Jeri his undivided attention. Jeri continued.

"It began one winter. Then lasted another. Now they act as if they own this place and everyone in it. My brother isn't a toy."

The Impresario rubbed his left ear and tugged at his goatee. He flexed his metallic limbs—an innovation of the Blueboys' hi-tech—until he rose exactly to Jeri's eye level. Then he rocked forward, maintaining his balance on the thin stilts.

"These days, we speak about it in a more, ah, veiled manner. Because of the bad boys, you know. And the woman who leads them."

"Not me. I'm tired of pretending."

"Many of us are," said The Impresario. "But..."

"But nobody fights it."

"Would you be shocked, my boy, if I told you that I'd talked with friends who feel the same way? People who consider the treatment of your brother as symbolic of how terrible things have gotten. They want footage. They would like to write articles and petition the governments in Sao Paolo and Washington."

"Talk won't get him back."

"What if they had documented proof?" said Skaff.

Jeri raised his eyebrows. "What do you mean?"

"What if certain, you know, sources had a clue to where Eric was? And perhaps had the means for a rescue.

Or at least for getting some of their, ah, indiscretions on film."

"You're talking about guerrillas, Skaff. I thought you were against getting involved?"

The man puffed up. "Yeah, maybe."

Jeri weighed Skaff's offer against his need for rest. He felt tired and dirty and groggy from the psychomists, yet a desire to retaliate burned inside him.

"What kind of force? Just a distraction, or enough men to meet the Blueboys head to head?"

The Impresario said, "Now, it might be a mistake to anger them. You've seen what they can do."

Maybe The Impresario believed what he'd said in the heat of speech, about a need for change, but his opinions went just so far. It was obvious he feared the Blueboys. Jeri wondered if this was even the same man from his teenage years, the kindly, fastidious gentleman who adored chess and reminisced about his days as a peace-keeper on the southern Pampas rangelands. He would be no help. Still, Jeri doubted Skaff could be useful either. The smuggler owned resources and men, no doubt, but he couldn't be counted on. He was a drug trader, and as such a one-dimensional man.

But then, could Jeri be choosey?

"Okay. Clue me in."

"Shall we talk someplace in private? There are details." Skaff looked about the Commons.

"Eric's room," Jeri said. Then, "How much of my savings will this cost?"

Skaff shrugged. "Cloaking devices and lasers don't come cheap."

03

Eric sensed that he lay flat, but only as a blind man senses the size and textures of the space about him. What he saw were things that did not exist. Or, actually, did not yet exist.

Weighty kong sloths. Toy jaguars the size of a man's hand. A toucan whose beak shined with its own light. Trees the height of skyscrapers. Butterflies that lived off decaying flesh. Frogs that imitated brilliant mosses. Carnivorous mosses that in turn imitated those brilliant frogs. Fish of every imaginable perversion. Crocodiles large enough to swallow a motorized vehicle whole. Invisible stinging wasps that drove the unwary mad.

Visions bloomed for him and took hold.

And when Eric had answered every question that the scientists could ask, undergone ten hours of brain scans and mind probes, suffered drugs that coursed his veins and quickly ebbed, they delivered his tired body to the Blue Queen in her private quonset at the fringe of the compound. The hut smelled of orchids. A late afternoon breeze blew through the end windows, and Berkey offered him a drink while she changed into a nightgown that covered her synthetic skin in diaphanous folds.

Eric sat on her bed as she rubbed her hips against him. She dragged her hollowed fingernails down his arms and back as she undressed him. The light scratches flared with E-pheromones, and he found renewed energy; he shivered with sexual tension that caused his groin to tighten and ache for release. He reached for her. She escaped him.

Eric chased the Blue Queen, but she danced out of reach with power-augmented ease and laughed as he tripped himself over furniture and stumbled against walls.

She squeezed her arms together and jutted her breasts at him. Bared the twin halves of her ass. At last, she allowed herself to be caught and dragged to bed, and there she whispered in his ear, urged him to take her roughly, to vent his frustration on her. He entered her with a cry, and though Eric hurried his passion, hoping to reach the quick release that would free him, she dampened the sensory centers of his brain with drugs that sent cold tendrils up the backs of his legs and along his spine. Her extended nails gouged his buttocks. Three times she shuddered with pleasure, while he slapped himself against her on the brink of orgasm. A brink that he never could tumble over.

And when he was too exhausted to continue, to take her once more into pleasure, she held him. Stroked his head. Asked him questions he could not refuse to answer. And answer again.

ଓ

At twilight on the evening of Eric's abduction, two airboats packed with armed men emerged from the dark tunnel of a canal-like igarapee and eased out along the shadowy edge of a large stretch of the Pantanal. Jeri squeezed into the bow of one airboat, content to let more experienced hands command the raid. His pilot was a fisherman, while a cocky little man named Vaqui—a leader of the insurgents—sat in the pilot's seat of the second boat. They cruised at a speed which allowed no more than a hum to echo across the water's surface, and they pulled alongside a small island dominated by two giant trees.

Jeri consulted with Vaqui through the distorting shimmer of the cloaking devices. Their voices wavered.

"You say the base is about three tenths of a kilometer more?"

"Yes," Vaqui said as his image warped toward Jeri. "The Blues call it D Base. There's nothing strategic or crucial about it, just an experimental center for engineering new strains of swamp life. But we suspect they experiment on people here too. Anyways, it's small, if Skaff 's sources are correct."

Jeri stared at their crude map. "So no hoverchops."

"Not usually, those stay at the airbase. But we expect one with General Berkey there."

"Why for Berkey?"

"Our intelligence contact says there's few more powerful than her in the entire military."

"Won't that mean more soldiers?"

"Maybe not. They're fairly cocky about their superiority."

"And?"

Vaqui frowned and tugged at his camouflage hat. "Sorry, I've been avoiding some unpleasant news. Our contact said that she uses the base as a lover's rendezvous. A place to meet your brother. So we're expecting slack security."

"Eric?" Jeri pushed his mouth in a sarcastic twist. "I don't believe it."

"I doubt he's a willing partner."

"My god!" Jeri stood and shook his fist at Vaqui. "What are we waiting for? Why did you keep that from me?"

"We couldn't let you go off half-cocked. A raid takes a cool head and absolute secrecy."

"And dumb-ass patience," Jeri's pilot added. "I don't move our butts until I know our diversion has worked. You might as well chill it."

Jeri stood and paced in a tight circle through volunteers that checked their guns or sat and smoked. He wondered what else these people had kept from him. It made him pound his forehead in frustration. "I'm trying to understand why no one told me."

"Because you'd have done what you're doing now."

Jeri didn't hear Vaqui. Insects bit him through his sweat-soaked clothes. His beard stubble itched. He muttered and fidgeted until a woman guerrilla sat him down, lit a cigarette for him. The others on the boat talked to him.

"Screw off!" he yelled at them.

Then the radio packet beeped on Vaqui's belt, a prearranged signal that meant another force of raiders had begun a harassment of Base C, twenty kilometers west of their position. Jeri picked out a lasrifle with a grenade launcher from an armory box recessed in the deck, then kneeled, his eyes fixed ahead.

☙

Eric stirred on the Blue Queen's great round bed, and he found himself spread-eagled again. The night was hot, without the breezes that had preceded dusk. Walls seemed to close in, seemed to tower and bend over him. Ugly thoughts flapped in his head like faceless bats. He rolled over and covered his head with a pillow. Visions continued.

Somewhere bright flashes clawed through the vines and fronds of the jungle, and two insectoid hoverchops

41

rose above the canopy to spin about and cast more light. One hoverchop skidded in a crash when it dove too close to the enemy. A Blueboy radio call went out across the Pantanal for help.

Eric's own call stirred shadows in the jungle. Jaguars stopped licking their paws in the trees. Tapirs snorted and pulled back in their bunkers of dirt and decaying debris. Boas coiled tighter about their limbs.

Across the dark acidic waters, the caimans and jacares gathered in groups along the igarapees and within the open water courses where the water didn't stagnate. Mutated ones, the immense lizards that the Blueboys tampered with as they had with Eric, clacked their jaws. Eyes glowed like coals above the waterline. These were the beasts that had haunted his dreams, yet now he saw them as possible allies. And the face of the largest one was human and familiar to him, achingly familiar.

"Eric. I'm coming for you," it said.

The lizard lost substance, shrunk, and floated to the ceiling. Whispering his name. Eric whimpered and pulled the pillows tight around his head. The Blue Queen rolled over and held him against her until the shaking subsided.

"What's wrong?" she asked.

She rubbed his back, then her touch inched down his buttocks until she reached his legs. Her fingers, with nails retracted, stroked his loose scrotum until it contracted.

Eric tried to block it out.

Tried not to respond to her coarse tongue moving across his belly, then coaxing him hard again.

ͽ

At first, no spotlights flooded the compound, so Jeri donned an infrared helmet and used the scope on his rifle to monitor the combat soldiers as they geared-up. The spots flicked on when the troopers boarded the hover-chop on the landing pad. With a roar, the vehicle lifted above D Base with its running lights winking in red and blue. It froze in the sky for a moment, then zipped away toward C Base, its air rotors churning the forest canopies below it like a hurricane.

Vaqui and the other pilot started their air foils at the height of the hoverchop's vertical rev up, and they gunned their way toward the base with their cloaking fields on. They traveled under a blackout, used the base as a homing target, and for a moment Jeri felt over-whelmed by its lights, seeing a pattern in their brilliance, a prophecy of death like the one he had sensed at Serra Pelada.

The boats hit the shallows and water splashed across Jeri's chest and under his visor, forcing him to think only of the moment, of the precise maneuvers they must exe-cute. They skimmed up on a grassy strip. Both pilots cut the cloaking with their engines, saving them for retreat. With infrared helmets tracking for movement, the raiders bailed out on the grass. From the top of Jeri's machine, the pilot cut the bowels out of two dish communication antennae with a small built-on laser cannon, then the cannon tipped skyward, a beacon of fiery neon, as the man tumbled forward.

Blood on the man's khakis. Red laser light darting around them. Two more men fell as Jeri sprinted toward a row of quonsets.

Ball lightning materialized about the raiders, lashing out with random threads of electricity. A Blueboy in a jetpack arced toward the ground about twenty meters in front of them, positioning himself to cut Jeri down, but Jeri heard the whistle of his descent, guessed the trajectory, and laid out a rifle grenade. The soldier crumbled as he landed, his chest smoking with a hole deep enough to bury a fist.

The voice called to Eric once more while he positioned himself on his knees and entered the Blue Queen from behind. He mumbled an obscenity. Shook his head.

"What's wrong?" she asked. This time she disengaged and snapped the lights on. "What is it?"

An alarm buzzed from her helmet on the bed stand, and she consulted someone through its speaker-remotes before unslinging her lasrifle and moving to the door.

In his mind, Eric envisioned someone in the shadows approaching the hut. An ally she would kill.

It took every ounce of strength in Eric to lift her pistol from its holster on the bedpost and follow the Blue Queen outside with it. It weighed tons, or seemed to. Differences mattered little to him.

Jeri sprinted for the end quonset, a fine vantage to command, but when he rounded the building he collided full-force with a Blueboy in a nightgown. The woman lost her weapon, staggered, yet kicked out and shattered Jeri's helmet and visor, sending him into a sprawl. He rolled onto his back. By then she'd poised her leg, heel pointed, to crush his nose and face. But a figure materialized from the doorway of the hut behind her.

❧

With both hands, Eric pressed the barrel of the hand laser to the back of the Blue Queen's skull. "No!" he shouted.

She hesitated, and the man on the ground rolled away from her and leveled his rifle before she could make a move for Eric's gun.

"Freeze, Berkey."

The Blue Queen lowered her leg and stood still. The man whipped off the remains of his helmet, kicked her weapon into the brush. With the situation changed, and his gun where she could grab it, Eric panicked. Flung the weapon away. Saw it bounce between the quonset's stilt pilings and slide into the shadows underneath.

"You have me at a disadvantage," she said to the man. Her voice dripped with superiority and pouting sensuality.

The man spat at her. "No more than you've had my brother."

With that, the world spun in Eric's head, and he collapsed against a tree stump. The voice was JERI's. His brother found him. His brother JERI had come home.

❧

Jeri considered Eric's state and how few power moves it would take for the General to lock him in a death grip. He stepped between them and backed Berkey away by several meters. She didn't blink once.

"I haven't hurt Eric."

"Sure, just look at him."

45

Jeri watched Berkey's face as she studied Eric where he lay, and his finger relaxed on the trigger when he saw how her eyes softened with a touch of regret.

"Oh, Eric. You knew this would happen. Didn't you?"

A spurt of adrenalin made his head explode with heat. He saw deeper. He sensed the truth behind her concern. She probed Eric, trying to sway him to admit to and use the psi powers he'd kept hidden, to give her concrete evidence to twist for her own purposes. Even with her life on the line, Berkey played for higher stakes. Mind control.

"What will you do with me, then?" she asked Jeri. Her words were coy, suggestive.

"You'll make a valuable prisoner."

Her smile turned feral. Her nails extended and retracted reflexively. "You assume that you'll take this base. Even without communications we will crush you. We're elite warriors, not rag-tag mercenaries."

"Shut up. You're in no position to bargain."

"On the contrary. If you don't surrender now, I'll have you both killed."

"We may be anyway."

She smoldered. "I didn't expect to see you again so soon, though when I did, I thought it would be different."

She eased toward him, moving her body with sinuous grace, jutting her chest ahead of her. He stared; the heat rose in him, intoxicating him. Jeri blinked rapidly. He remembered how she'd marked him with the E-pheromones, and his heat turned to rage. He shook with the urge to kill her.

"Move slowly," he said in a growl. "Toward the hut."

She shifted her weight, stepped to the door in a rigid goosestep. Bracing his lasrifle in his armpit, Jeri raised Eric with one arm and followed her inside just as a lightning ball crackled over the roof. She searched the bare floor, as if discerning a message in the pattern of knots and holes in the boards, and then sat in a specific spot. Jeri saw nothing alarming about this behavior. It seemed engineered to confuse him, to throw him off. He let Eric collapse on the bed and moved opposite Berkey to wait for a lull in the firefight. He'd deal with her when it was time to make a run for the boats.

The door burst open. Jeri glanced briefly to the intruders, but held his aim steady on the woman.

"Jeri!" The voice belonged to Vaqui.

"What's happened?"

"We've routed the base. The lightning weapons must have attracted the big crocs, the monster ones. They're eating Blueboys and ignoring us. It's incredible. Many have deserted their positions. We've bolted the leftovers in the lab freezers and reinforced the doors."

Berkey showed no expression.

"Not her, though," the guerrilla said. "We blow her away. Without a leader, the Blueboys can't organize a retaliation."

"What about the video footage on their labs? Proof of what they're doing here?"

Vaqui laughed. "The film never mattered, really. We've hurt them and freed a comrade. Imagine how much press that will get. Something to rally around. That is if we get our asses out of here."

"My brother needs help."

Jeri stood and slung his rifle over his shoulder, and he pulled Eric to his feet just as Berkey made a blitzkrieg move. She smashed her hand through the floor, grabbed Eric's pistol—which she'd determined to be there by some special method of sensing—and then fired as she vaulted for the end window. Vaqui took a shoulder hit. The frame shattered before her and sprayed glass through the room; Berkey was gone. Jeri made Eric run before him out the door.

Near the waterfront, Vaqui's men carried the wounded. An airboat started and backed out into the swamp just as the hoverchop returning from C Base showed over the tree line and hung in the air above the fight, unsure about landing and, no doubt, unsure as to what was going on. It pumped laser fire, but too late to be effective. The boat retreated with its cloak on.

Jeri let Eric fall in the grass while yelling for someone to help him, then he sprinted for the second airboat that stayed hidden by a low overhanging tree. Red beams cut the dirt a meter to his right. He climbed over several wounded on stretchers at the bow and swung into the pilot's seat in a fluid motion. He righted the laser cannon and flipped on the image screen. It worked; the battery pack hadn't burned out when the original gunner had been hit. He spun the cannon without its automatic targeting and slammed the fire toggle three, four times.

Jeri flinched as a pulsing sensation ran into his hands. A thick beam cut past the tree limbs and disappeared to the right of the hoverchop. Then another, closer in. Another. The hoverchop homed in with a return volley that set the leafy cover afire and seared the hair on the side of his face. Jeri jerked the beam left as the last shot discharged and heard a thump-and-roar as the hoverchop exploded into streamers of sizzling metal. The men hooted in celebration, but small arms fire continued to pump past them from somewhere in the jungle. A few of Vaqui's boys answered. Then a canister of psychomist burped in the shallows to their rear, an ineffective shot smothered by the water.

Vaqui dragged Eric on board and then collapsed beside him on the deck. Two stragglers sprayed light fire as they stood at the bow. Eric cut a couple swaths with the canon until a replacement pilot moved him from the seat. They pulled out, gun barrels aglow from repeated firing, and no one answered their barrage as the cloaking field flickered on and the rotors kicked up spray. In the receding glow of the spotlights, a swarm of crocodiles queued up beyond the quonsets and moved off into the jungle. Jeri heard screams. He thought he saw one beast the size of a tank raise its jaws and shake the body of a Blueboy like a ragdoll. Somehow, as if Eric's gift coursed through him, he knew it was the soldier named Trigger.

After making Eric comfortable, Jeri moved alongside Vaqui and pointed to the shore while he helped him bandage his shoulder. They watched as the base shrunk to a blob of light.

"They won't be happy over losing that hoverchop," Jeri yelled over the motor noise. "Or the men."

"Doesn't matter. We hurt them bad enough that they can't strike hard. Not immediately." Vaqui shook his head. "Wish I'd killed the woman. That would have been a blow!"

"Maybe."

Jeri tuned Vaqui out yet continued to bandage him. The man's bloodthirsty attitude didn't ring true with the original agreement on their objectives. Suddenly he felt alone, and it occurred to Jeri that this was how he'd begun the adventure: cruising one-way through Blueland, soaked to the bone, and hollering over the sound of an engine to someone he had every reason to mistrust.

The pilot eased off on the gas and turned toward an inlet.

愈

The boat levitated above the water. It seemed to Eric that he was transported on heavenly breath into a featureless gap between two dark throne-like swamp trees, then onto an open, flat island. Their ascension came to an abrupt halt. Voices cried out. Urged them to get the wounded off, guided by the cyclops eye of a single flashlight.

"So you got him," a fat man said as he clicked out the light and helped Eric from the boat with his brother. Eric heard the excitement in the men's voices in the dark, and it seemed also to be bubbling from within him and spilling back through everyone.

"Skaff. What are you doing here?" Jeri said.

"Offering you alternative transport. The boats aren't safe. We've got an ultralite plane."

Eric lost himself in the sound of the voices, the flow of syllables that issued from a timeless dimension that engulfed them.

"We? Since when did you join the guerrillas?"

"I never left. I was a part of it all along. Delivering the letter, playing reluctant to help unless I got my profits. And backing the lie about publicity footage and attacking the Blues in the press. The whole bit. Sorry. Our leader thought it best."

A half-man materialized from a swarm of figures busy in the near dark about them. Eric's friend and confident. Secret leader of the guerrilla forces. He embraced Eric, and as he did, Eric saw the shock in his brother's face. His brother felt the sting of betrayal.

The Impresario said, "I'm glad we got you out, son."

Jeri pushed The Impresario away from him, and Eric sensed wild tension. Angry frisson.

"I got him out." Jeri spat. "I don't need help any more. Not from you. You planned it all without including me. You put Eric's life on the line."

"All of ours are on the line. That's what it means here, Jeri. You've been away too long to see how desperate things have become. Our time draws near. We can't turn away."

"Shit! Cut the propaganda crap."

"As you wish," The Impresario said as he bowed. "We can argue later. Right now you *do* need us."

Eric followed the loping werewolf stride of The Impresario across a moonlit glade, and the man strapped Eric into a stripped down airplane built for four. He and Jeri did the same. The man called Skaff stopped next to Jeri and leaned close.

"Things may get hot, still. If the Blues retaliate tonight, we have people ready to resist."

"Why risk it? They won't be surprised a second time."

"Ah, but a real battle would draw media attention across the globe."

Skaff slapped Jeri on the back and settled himself at the nose. He started the engine. They slid into the darkness, lifting out over the water and the forest dappled with pale moonbeams. The Impresario dangled his glittering bionic legs like a fisherman trolling, hoping, perhaps, to catch his fate. Eric felt transformed. Veins iridescent.

Cʒ

Jeri sensed a tug at his shoulder, and he bent until his forehead was resting against his brother's.

"Jer?" Eric's eyes were big.

Jeri ran his fingers through Eric's hair and forced a smile, relieved that he no longer needed to keep his adrenalin pumping.

"Don't worry," Eric said. His face softened. "She won't touch us. I know this."

"Did you call up the caimans against her?" he asked Eric. "Did you *know* to do that?"

"Yes." Eric smiled feebly. "I'm sorry. That's what she wanted, wasn't it? For me to expose what Mama calls my gift."

"Yes. But she got more than she bargained for. Eh?"

Eric mumbled. He fell off to sleep.

Though time had become elastic for him during the raid, throwing off his sense of the hour, a feeling of surprise tingled through Jeri's nerves as the morning sun rose, arced over the trees, then eclipsed. Another streaked ahead, its actinic light bathing the leafy canopy below. Skaff cheered while The Impresario called out the locations of firefights in Caceres and along the edges of the swamp, rocking the plane with gleeful idiocy, and as the true extent of The Impresario's manipulations dawned on Jeri, the truth of how he'd been used, Jeri barked a laugh.

It didn't matter that his brother was just a spark to blow the keg, an excuse for an uprising. He didn't care about their lies to him. Or their hidden motives, which as he suspected now, could be reduced to self-interest and guilt for Skaff, and revenge for The Impresario. And Jeri didn't want to think about how simply they had subverted him. How gullible he'd been. How easily they'd exploited his own guilt and anger from the moment they found him at the gold mine.

He cared only that he had Eric. No more, no less.

The sky danced with light, and explosive echoes skipped across the water and bounced up from the canopied islands. Eric awoke against Jeri's shoulder. He began to sob. Jeri tried to cry with him, to share release, but he found his emotions steeled against it. They weren't free of Blueland yet. He held Eric close and watched as Skaff led them like a madman, yelling and dipping the plane and transporting them into a future that burst with possibilities new and important.

VISIONS

PRELUDE
Boston/Frazier

Some say that more than a century
has passed since the Radiation Wars,
if they were wars and not merely
an avalanche of terrorist abandon.

Others claim time as we knew it
has expired, that we now inhabit
a single day stretched beyond all
limits, where our theorems have
decayed to intangibles we are
no longer capable of grasping.

They contend we are living in
the protracted afternoon of
our species, our perceptions
and understandings changing
at random with the mercurial
winds that stream across
a fearsome dark continent

From the Petén jungle, down
the Isthmus to the Amazon
and beyond, spanning the
land's breadth and stretching
as far south as the Pantanal
that swallows old Paraguay
and half of Argentina, change
has become the only constant.

Except for a few resistant trees
and the immutable cockroach,

this world could be the province
of a being wholly supernatural,
some raging demon in exile.

In those rare human enclaves
that survive along the coasts,
natives have raised effigies to
a creature half anima, half ego.
A few of the learned, inspired
by divine revelation or delusion,
worship more private idols.
None of us are sure of the truth.

Yes, there are those who believe
there are answers to be found.
They travel here from the North,
from the surviving dome cities
where older ways are preserved.
The cycled air in their sealed habitats
runs through their blood and lungs.
What can they possibly understand?

The Mutant Forest guards its secrets,
not by camouflage but by alteration,
certainties transformed to deceits.
The sheet lightning that ignites our
horizon may presage a coming storm,
or be only a contrary precursor to dusk.

A CAUTIONARY NOTE TO TRAVELERS THROUGH THE MUTANT RAIN FOREST

Frazier

If you run deep within the gloomy fringe
where black mahoganies are upright spades
that shudder, shift and moan like ghostly shades,
be wary then of creatures fresh of tinge.
The *necrophida* moths grow huge as planes,
and feast on corpses hung in cauls of moss.
The *kongii* sloths will make the treetops toss
to shape unearthly music from the rains.
And blue *duendes* shriek along your trail,
those shadow monkeys slick and dark as oil
who'll brave a ring of fires that lick and boil
to steal your soul; you'll flee to no avail.
Their stares can bristle full with spikes of light.
On them transfixed you'll spend eternal night.

THREE EVOCATIONS
OF THE MUTANT RAIN FOREST
Boston

Evolution

When young Charles rode the Beagle round the Cape
bound for the revelations of the Galapagos,
little did he know that war and rampant
radiation would turn this continent
he circumnavigated into a land
which would first prove his
theories of survival
and selection,
not in millennia but months,
and with like rapidity prove them
as useless as Newton's linear equations
to the curving temporal attenuations of space.
And now even his special island is rife
with protean life and the unique
and isolated species he once
cataloged with such care
have vanished
in an onslaught far more
unique and constantly changing,
more fertile than flights of pure imagination.

Expansion

From space, with each revolution of the planet,
the dark arboreal palimpsest seems to lengthen.
In the time lapsed motion of satellite tapes,
it swells like a gargantuan amoeba in mitosis.
Rio. Caracas. Sao Paulo. The coastal cities

which survive do so by a daily confrontation.
The lines of armor clad troops advance warily,
spraying gouts of liquid fire into the wilds.
Napalm. Cyanogen. Agent Orange. A poison rain
of defoliants and excoriation falls in waves
from the decks of combat planes and choppers,
yet the flames are strangely dampened and die.
In a makeshift refugee camp, a native Indio
from the abandoned interior, drafted to fight,
sleeps in battle fatigues by his pregnant wife.
All his dreams have been transformed to frights
in which the serpentine vines he burns by day
have rooted deep within their displaced lives,
to twine and strangulate the bloody umbilical
and suffocate the breath of his unborn child.

Elan Vital

Beyond the claws of bestial battle,
beyond the green on green attrition,
some say a force is dwelling here
which links its manifold creations,
a rank and raging barbaric spirit,
a dim but still awakening sentience,
which touches and taints our souls
and gives rise to stray obsessions.
The banks of thunderous cumuli
stacked against the Andes range,
fall east to meet miasmic mists
which rise in streaming drifts
from the swamps of lowland basins,
and in this airborne compilation
dense and brackish figures evolve

in an endless surreal cinemontage
of unconscious organic visions.
Some say that far and farther south
beyond the Rivers Negro and Parana,
beyond the encroaching vegetation,
a retreating tribe has suffered
an enchantment and possession
in the shadow of the forest wall,
for now they divinate its growth
and foretell our changeling future
as they read the clouds' collisions.

TRACKING THROUGH
THE MUTANT RAIN FOREST
Frazier

In the twilit ceibas above our camp,
here on the edge of the Mutant Rain Forest,
a neon toucan cycles light;
it blends with other birds that blink like
constellations in the forest canopy.

Genna points to a log mossy with
lapis bees dueling lime ants.
The foxfire toads glow like golden fungi
while a row of wood mushrooms mimics them
in turn, poisoning one for its nutrients.

Even some of the cloud pools, ringing
us like the footprints of the monster
we track, are not what they seem—
tiny tongues of quicksilver lapping
at the profusion of growth and decay.

Further up the emerald mountain, Jorge has
found a freshly slaughtered jaguar already
veined over with a netting of blood-root.
Our quarry may still be far ahead, reminds Genna.
I shrug and stir our bubbling pot of mate.

At night in our tents we listen,
sweating and burning as with fever,
to the jungle toss and turn.
Genna whispers, how, how can we find him?
Sleep presses on us like a weight.
In dreams, I know that Genna is right;

a vision sputters like a volcano in my head.
Far ahead, wreathed in ethereal light,
a path winds into a lost horizon where only
new creatures—of a new bestiary—may follow.

At dawn Genna stirs and rubs against me.
I hold her, drowsy and disoriented.
From high on the mist-shrouded mountain,
an unearthly cry rises like a breeze
and fades with the last dregs of night.

NIGHT FISHING
ON THE CARIBBEAN LITTORAL
Boston/Frazier

Out beyond a humid sluggish slip of coast where
mangrove cays nose under like scuttled battleships,
beyond the corrugated tin hovels where Obeah ladies
stir their gruely brews of blue magic on to dawn,
beyond the hanging carcasses of loggerheads and crocs
yellowing to decay in the moon's carious light,
a patch of the Mutant Rain Forest shudders lifelike
in the wake of a tropical squall, spooking the Caribs
who night fish from a rickety stilt-legged pier,
causing them to blow their morning conches
and pipe a dire revelry to the dark wind above.

I've heard a Carib whisper of stunted *duendes*,
hairy four-fingered throwbacks who fly the canopy,
fleeting as ghosts, and "cut de t'umbs of de unwary"
because "dey so bad wanna be like us, mon."
I have listened to tales of the *woohli's* immense jaws,
enough to swallow a jaguar whole, or whole men,
or "scoop de manatees" into its barrel belly by threes;
yet these are common mutations, Campe insists
as we motor past jumbled slag heaps of broken coral
to navigate the verdant delta of the Rio Mysterioso.

This handsome mestizo who trails a feathered streamer
from his cayuca speaks to me of the dreadful *dagon*
who can mimic any creature, who ensnares its prey
by casting a spectral net of temporal dissociation,
I imagine other *bête noires* myself, forms fearsome
in their unbounded multiplicity, a raft of shadowy

anti-lives beyond the tenets of biology or reason
rising from the depths of our shared animal dreams.

Campe's fantasies lull me with their lyric cadence,
and we leave the Mysterioso and wind through channels
beneath a recent growth of red *gargantua* leaves,
amidst interlocking root chains of walking *socratea*,
around several culs-de-sac and into a broad lagoon.
His lilting tongue casts my thoughts into a trance
bound by damp pulses of heat and the ancient echoes
of conquistadors, of rum captains and mahogany runners.
The dead reel past in a gritty sanguine rush
to bare the bones of avarice, the veins of disease,
still bedrock deep in the soil of this changing land.

Suddenly I am transfixed by a reflection on the water,
one that freezes my every muscle in cataleptic thrall:
Campe's rippling moon-made image does not shine true,
but resembles the spread of a transfigured starfish,
floating up towards me and grasping, writhing in its
fluid moment like a great, severed, many-fingered hand.

NIGHTS WITH GENNA'S FIELD JOURNALS
Frazier

She rises through the low branches with difficulty
the rope swaying as she kicks off mossy trunks
the ascending device ratcheting slowly
she looks toward the leafy green heavens
and shoots one-handed with the vidcam

> *The Least Bird of Paradise, transparent*
> *save for its milky breast and bones.*
> *And for the faintest pink of its blood.*
> *It picks at lemon beetles and ruby bees.*

High in the canopy the sleeping platform sways
the wind moving even the thickest trees
evening approaches and the rains abate
the sun breaks beneath the leaden cloud cover
caught in the moisture that beads her skin
and turns to jewels of blood on a lizard's back

> *The setting sun slithers on the Mirror Owls*
> *as they reflect the full spectrum*
> *of rainbowed helliconia and lianas.*

Genna slips into the cocoon of her hammock
under the veils of useless bug netting
and writes by flashlight in her book

> *An iridescent ibis eclipses all*
> *color with its phosphor-bright bill.*

One thing puzzles her in these nocturnal musings
a quandary about the future of changeling fauna

life on the turn of such strange tides

> *What changes are wrought in the world?*
> *How far and how fundamental?*
> *For now the females are brightest plumed,*
> *wraiths flitting across the twilight airglow.*

**_THE RAIN THAT FALLS
IN THE MUTANT RAIN FOREST_**
Boston

The rain that falls
in the Mutant Rain Forest
is nothing like the rain
that falls to the North,
speckling the dome cities
and sprinkling the parched
wastelands with sparse droplets.
The rain that falls to the North
can be forecast after a fashion,
as rain has always been forecast.

The rain that falls
in the Mutant Rain Forest
can never be forecast.
One second you will spy
the sky above, a pure azure
blue through the leafy canopy.
You will spot snatches of the
brightly burning sun among
the limbs overhead and see
how it dapples the forest floor
with patches of light and shadow.
The next instant your world
can darken as the heavens
turn to a swirling gray mass
and lightning crackles and
roaring sheets of water
come pounding down
upon you with a force

that steals your breath away,
a crushing weight that will
drop you to your knees.

The rain that falls
in the Mutant Rain Forest
does not smell like the rain
that falls to the North,
acidic and clogged
with particulate matter,
reeking with the foul
stench of chemical waste,
a rain that can carry pox
and typhoid and cholera.

The rain that falls
in the Mutant Rain Forest
smells rich and pungent
with organic material,
quenching the insatiable
thirst of the forest and
impregnating it with the
seeds of further change,
intoxicating the forest with
its sustenance and vitality,
filling the forest with
endless possibilities,
phantasmagoric
and more delirious
than fevered dreams
or mad hallucinations.

The rain that falls

in the Mutant Rain Forest
is bracing and laced
with tempting flavors
you can't quite place,
yet boil thoroughly
or drink sparingly,
unless you wish
to join the forest
in its endless travails
and transformations.

METEOROLOGICAL RECKONING
IN THE MUTANT RAIN FOREST
Frazier

The vast seasonal fall of rains
upon the Mutant Rain Forest
shapes a recurring climate cycle,
a self-contained vortex that deposits
moisture deep into its cloud banks.
Spanning the core to outer limbs,
a complex ecosystem thrives within,
a hierarchy from protozoa to nanofrogs
to boat-sized water striders who sense
the vibrations of evaporative change
across the woodlands below and steer
the weather mass by innate science.

Sometimes the yin and the yang
of exogenetic forces require
a tweak, a modification, a tailoring,
then the rains fall heavy with
chemical mutagens and biotic juju.
Sometimes the rains are pure and
sweet as the nectar of canopy flowers.
Sometimes in a severe flood interval,
when the rivers flush the detritus
then recede to their original banks,
fresh protean life forms push ashore to
breathe the humid air of regeneration.

A DECADENT ROMANTIC AFFLICTED BY THE MUTANT RAIN FOREST

Boston

You sit beside the inaudible whir
of your holodeck in the air-conditioned
darkness and you watch the colors

immerse the cube in their constant flowing,
their constant reversals and refrains,
you watch as the impossible landscape

with its impossible fauna and flora
materializes before your curious gaze,
and though you know and know again

full well of artful holographic fakes,
though all the reason in your chest
denies the being of this nightmare world

of unreined beauty and extravagant pain,
a shiver passes across your perception
and snags at the borders of your brain,

and though you turn away to select
another disc, to adjust the thermostat,
to light illegal smoke or take another

sip of something soothing and mundane,
to caress yourself or an imaginary lover
as the holos in your cube become profane,

the visions you have witnessed still remain,
to halt your dreams, to stalk your reveries,
to arise unbidden in the midden of your life

and billow the fabric of your middling days,
like a mystery laden with darkling runes
and windswept afternoons of sun and rain.

LUMINOUS DECAY
Frazier

Clues to their shadowy residency
Are numerous on the overgrown estate
Broken plaster on the upper floors
Edged with the stab marks of pencils
Toothbrushes frozen upright
In glass jars of hardened paint
Aligned by the west entrance
Also down in the sunken lands
Fishing lines tied to hammers
Then strung into reed-choked ponds

The feral young speak a jungle patois
Born of happenstance
French plus aristocratic Spanish
Plus made-up words or sounds
That they all understand
Punctuated by panther calls
The girls dress up from moldy trunks
Left in the staff quarters below
Then discard their fashion at will
Make togas of their bed sheets
The boys mimic schooling in a study
Papered with simple portraits
Of what they once called
The Vast Governess Parade

The old Portuguese cook soldiers on
For them with great affection
She raids the wall safes
Fills up the house larder

Feeds the young with stews
Porridges fragrant breads jams
These are left in white bowls
On the landings of the grand staircase
By the cook's mute son
Whom the girls tease mercilessly
Before they use him roughly
To discover gambling or sex
He must also tend to Her Ladyship
Who is bed-ridden but lucid
In her demands and her sorrows

Sometimes a traveler materializes
Usually scared off by the burned ruin
Of much of the east wing
Those few that brave the front entrance
Are feted in the dining room
With teas and bright talk
Of the decline of the great families
Or the mutations outside their home
This is the one room kept tidy
And polished by everyone but the mute
Who keeps to his unending chores
And the whims of women

At night the young haunt
The garden pathways in games
That sport a savage jungle logic
Then feed the old wolfhound
From tins and laugh sweetly
As they toss him a stick
Cut from the Lord's favorite cane

By morning they scatter
To their favorite dens or follies
Throughout the mapless grounds

Soon they will straighten their posture
Comb out their dreadlocks
Find respectable gear to wear
Pilfer the silver money box
Kiss Her Ladyship on the ring
Venture out to their scattered lives

Of course they will all return here
Busted by the travails of knowledge
They will bury each other's bones
Until the mute stands alone
Silent in the night rains

As the rooms are cleared of debris
The long lost inheritors of the estate
Will find his yellowed journals
Feverishly scribed
In an indecipherable language
Illustrated with countless line drawings
And vibrant watercolors
Of ethereal grace

GHOSTS DEVILS DEEP
IN THE MUTANT RAIN FOREST
Boston

Deep in the forest,
where the sun struggles
to pierce the canopy
of dank growth,
where the air is
dense and fetid,
eerie half-creatures
thrive and breed.

Amid bromeliads and molds,
angle hair mushrooms
and gnarled moss,
they rise up from
the rotting undergrowth,
flickering into and
out of existence.

One moment visible,
the next they vanish,
their molecules
stretched so thin
they are only wraiths,
ephemeral as illusions
of shadowed light
and the chemistry
of your eyes.

Our native guides
have dubbed them
diabo fantasmas,

whispering the words
beneath their breath
like a curse
or a benediction,
taking them
for lost souls
who have died here
without absolution.

HOLOS AT AN EXHIBITION
OF THE MUTANT RAIN FOREST

Bruce Boston & Robert Frazier

The scene within the cube of the sculpted holograph is both dim and cryptic. Shadow is heightened to the point where color has bled away. Only a few earth tones and the dullest of greens remain. In the foreground three figures crouch about a piece of equipment, obscuring its nature. Whatever their task, they are dwarfed to insignificance by the forest backdrop. Even in this dimness, the gargantuan trunks that rise about them, the tubular vines and elephantine branches are what claim the viewer's attention.

In one corner of the frame, a single patch of light has penetrated the dense canopy. As it breaks through the growth, the pattern it etches upon the leaves creates the illusion of a ghostly face, with wide-set eyes and lips compressed, silently watching the scene below.

ଔ

With light migrating to shadow, and strands of dusk filtering like smoke through the nearly opaque canopy of the Mutant Rain Forest, a least-bird of paradise lit on a cobalt liana above holographer Genna Opall, causing a stir among the Indios in the camp. One man cursed beneath his breath. Another began to mumble a stuttering incantation.

The natives thought the bird ugly, its bizarre transparency a sign of ill fortune. To Genna it was a creature of rare beauty, even more beautiful than the sum of its parts: bright bead eyes, a froth of diaphanous feathers, glassy flesh shot through with fragile bones, visibly flowing veins and capillaries. She identified with the least-bird. Not because of its appearance, but because it survived in this transformed Amazonia by the same strategies she used to navigate the world beyond. They both moved swiftly, shifting from other's sights. Both pursued a goal as elusive as themselves. The bird sought survival in a hostile and constantly changing environment. Genna sought a breakthrough in the cutthroat and constantly changing haut monde of modern art. Fusing holography with light sculpture on image-sensitive glass solids, she planned not only to create a revolutionary form but to establish her name and fortune.

Genna unzipped the case and eased out her camera. While she quickly thumbed in a new cartridge, Mingus Jahns, the heavyset leader of their party, calmed the Indio porters and raised his rifle. Seconds later the least-bird spooked when it heard the harsh trill of a siren eagle. Genna tried to track its sudden flight with her viewfinder. Mingus' shot rang through the small clearing, shattering a branch near where the bird had perched.

Genna tossed back her dark and tangled hair. She pivoted to face Mingus, hands on her hips, the holocam swinging at her waist. Anger smoldered in her eyes, but when she spoke her voice was even.

"That was a rare bird," she said. "You should have given me time for a photo."

Mingus wiped his forehead on the sleeve of his khaki shirt and smiled condescendingly. With his balding head, his untrimmed gray mustache, and the thick folds of flesh about his neck, he made her think of an aging walrus.

"Be kind to your host," he warned. "It was the eagle who scared the least-bird away. Not me."

"But you tried."

"According to the Indios, that bird brings bad luck."

Genna laughed. "And you believe them?"

"They know more about the forest than we do." Mingus' small features narrowed further. "Remember, Miss Opall, your job is to stay out of the way and take the photos you were hired to take...not to put together your next show."

Genna tugged at the gold loop in one ear and straightened the collar of her camouflage fatigues. She asked herself why she tolerated men like Mingus, and why so many were like him: self-centered, insensitive, lacking the ability to appreciate any needs other than their own. Just as they seemed lacking in any sense of wonder regarding the inexplicable changes taking place throughout the world...the strangest of all being the forest they now crossed. In this case she knew the answer. Since she lacked the funds to mount an expedition of her own, Mingus was her entree to this land she so desperately wanted to holograph.

"You're jealous," she said as the man turned his sweat-stained back on her and entered his tent.

"Jealous?" another voice asked. "Of what?"

It was their guide, Jorge, who knelt stirring the coals in a small circle of stones. Jorge dressed in black from head to foot and always carried himself with the rigid grace of a military man. More than once since their departure from the coast, Genna had caught his eyes upon her in a seemingly incurious stare. Yet he always glanced away as soon as his gaze was returned. She couldn't be sure if he were attracted to her, or merely judging the wisdom of bringing a woman, this particular woman, on their expedition.

"He's jealous of my career, of course."

Jorge removed his short-brimmed cap and ran one hand across his forehead, smoothing back his already slicked-down hair. In the shadows filling the clearing, his brows and thin mustache were so sharply etched against his pale Castilian features they could have been painted on.

"But he pays for this expedition, señorita. He pays you to take photographs of him, not of the birds. Perhaps it is you who are jealous of him."

"No!" Genna answered, venting her anger. "How could I be jealous of a man who relies on his wealth...and a gun...instead of his wits?"

"He is a successful man...a man of action. He acts on what the Indios tell him."

"You defend him," she said, "only because you allow him to treat you like dirt. That doesn't mean I will."

Jorge shrugged. "I have also been paid for a job. To guide us through a world where we do not belong. The jungle is our true enemy. We must learn not to fight among ourselves."

He replaced his cap squarely and turned back to his brew pot on its tripod over the coals, flipping back the lid to examine the maté simmering within. Genna expected nothing further from him, so she wandered off to the perimeter of the camp, where Paulo—Jorge's assistant—and two breech-clothed Indios were erecting a sonic projector that would offer protection against the lesser beasts of the night, and warn the sentries of the approach of anything larger.

☓

Gamboge. Aquamarine. Vermilion. Colors so brilliant that at first guess one would suspect they have been computer enhanced. Acid violet. Chartreuse. Neon blue. Colors so intense and multiple that at first glance they obscure the figures beneath, and the initial impression is that of an abstract sculpture, reminiscent of Harding, or Weiss' "Berlin Travesty."

It is only on closer examination that one can delineate a flock of birds, caught by the holo lens in mid-flight and full sunlight as they rise in startled flight from the brush. Despite the fact that no two are plumed alike, their common form and flock would indicate they are of the same species. The frame that surrounds them has been cast as a tetrahedron rather than a cube. Their flight leads not to the open heavens as one might expect, but to a foreshortened sky that narrows in steeply inclined planes to a single vanishing point.

☓

Next day, against Jorge's advice, Mingus decided they should move away from the Para River. He insisted they return to a cracked strip of pavement they had crossed the previous afternoon and follow its path deeper into the forest proper. According to their maps, dating from an era when civilization claimed this land, the pavement had at one time been a road, a tributary of the great Pan American Highway that was said to have spanned the length of the continent. Now its eroded track disappeared into dense growth.

Mingus' goal was to find the humani, a species so rare that Jorge and the Indios knew it by reputation only. He believed that this near-mythic creature—part cat, part man—had abducted his wife on a hunting trip more than a year before. Since then he had become obsessed. Rightly or wrongly, he was convinced that by finding the humani he would find his "beloved Therese," or at least some clue to her fate. From the distant domed city of Dallas, he had already commissioned many a South American tracker to no avail. Now he returned to take up the search with manic intensity. Jorge and the Indios he hired to guide and protect him; Genna to record the highlights of an odyssey that, at least in Mingus' mind, had taken on epic proportions.

Each night by their campfire, Mingus would unfold a plastic accordion of his wife's photos he carried in his shirt pocket. While he reminisced at length, in maudlin and idealized terms, of their unfaltering love for one another, he would force the photos upon his hirelings. Genna already knew Therese's face by heart, unexceptional but for its wide-set eyes, beautiful yet at the same time haunted, pale green eyes that reflected more than a fair share of suffering. No doubt the result, she concluded, of having to live with a man like Mingus Jahns.

An hour before dawn they broke camp and plunged into shadow. Paulo and two natives worked the front with long machetes, cutting back the barbed growth that overflowed the old highway. Although Jorge hovered close behind the trio, he seemed to command from a sullen distance. He stood tall in his black boots, a heavy machine pistol gripped in one hand and resting against his hip. Genna followed a few paces back, scanning the passing growth, alert for photo opportunities. Mingus and two more Indios, all carrying heavy packs and armed with automatic rifles and gas grenades, brought up the rear.

At this hour the forest remained immersed in sleep; neither the birds, nor monkey frogs, nor any of the other mutated animals in the overhanging canopy, intruded on the gloomy solitude. Except for the swish and hack of the machetes, and Jorge's low monosyllabic commands, an unnatural silence reigned about them. Yet within that silence, Genna sensed something more. A presence, grave and watchful, as if some invisible denizen were observing them from the brush. She shrugged off the feeling. Neither a veteran of the Mutant Rain Forest nor a stranger to it, she had already learned that this was a realm where imagination took flight. She knew there were dangers real enough without inventing more.

Trees of incredible girth rose about them and loomed over their heads. Deadwood stumps canted like quaint tombstones in an abandoned graveyard. Lianas hung everywhere in great tatters of lacework, some of them glowing faintly in the half light. In more open areas, where the canopy had been rent by fallen giants and sunlight had penetrated, the forest erected a lush vegetable fortress. Gnarled bamboo canes barricaded these wildlife rookeries, along with twenty-foot Spanish bayonets and multitudinous strains of rainbow-hued cacti. Here their machetes proved useless. They were forced to abandon the track of the old highway several times and circle back. Genna slapped and cursed aloud at the clouds of biting flies that paced their slow progress.

Suddenly, where only a ghostly pall had hung in the sky, the sun broke through. Morning light flooded the foliage and the forest came to life. Blue-bearded marmosets chattered as they leaped from branch to branch. The growth on every side looked faceted, as if it were made of jewels, and the dew, where it glittered on fallen leaves, shone like a sea of miniature stars beneath their feet. Genna snapped pictures furiously as a flock of iridescent ibises lifted from a clump of orange palmetto, their wings beating with increasing speed as they gained momentum.

☙

The man stands at cube center, not so much smiling for the camera as grimacing. A short and stocky man, dressed in khaki, beads of sweat glistening along the length of his receding brow, his features small and screwed tightly to his face. In one raised hand he grips a large machete, its curved blade catching the light and reflecting a single ray that lengthens and hangs suspended like an imperfection in the glass. He stands poised as if to strike the brush before him, but the stance is obviously posed, no blow about to be delivered.

The varied play of sun and shadow in the leaves at his back suggests a hundred and more incipient organic forms...a panther...a dragon...a man with arms akimbo, an uncoiling serpent rising up and about to strike...a pale green face, its darkened mouth stretched cave-like in the midst of a scream or exclamation.

☙

The air grew thick with heat and humidity, and Jorge slowed their pace. From far ahead, the low basso roar of a large animal sounded.

"Have we heard that before?" Genna asked.

Mingus stood by her side, thick hairy arms taut and his knuckles whitening upon the stock of his rifle.

"It's the humani," he said. "We've found it at last!"

Jorge shook his head.

"I wish we could see it," Genna mused. "I'd like to get something big on film."

Mingus grunted, pushing his way past Jorge on the narrow trail to order the men to chop faster. Paulo and the Indios looked to the Castilian, who nodded his assent.

"Señor, just so you understand...I give the orders."

Mingus bristled and straightened. "I'm paying a bloody fortune for this. If I want to move faster, then we'll damn well move!"

Genna sensed an electric silence settling about the two men as Jorge called their progress to a halt. More than ever his expression was etched in granite. It occurred to Genna that his distaste for Mingus might more than match her own.

Jorge gestured to the jungle before them. "If we follow you, Señor Jahns, then you can be the first one to die."

"Is that a threat?" Mingus began to lift his rifle, but Jorge blocked it with his arm and shoved it aside. He stepped in close, leaning down into the shorter man's reddening face.

"It's not a threat, señor. Only a fool would allow an inexperienced man to lead the way in this forest. And since you would follow yourself, you are a fool twice over. Out here, the reckless are the first to die. You step into arrow root and pfftt!"—he snapped his fingers next to Mingus' ear—"you are dead."

"All right, all right," Mingus said, though still standing his ground. "Just tell them to chop faster. We're losing our chance at the goddamn humani!"

Jorge stepped back and mockingly doffed his cap. The tension between the two men abated. "As you request, señor."

As they again pushed forward, with Mingus now trying to help the natives clear brush, Genna leaned toward Jorge. He tipped his head to let her close enough to whisper.

"I don't see what that accomplished," she said. "You're still taking his orders."

Jorge laughed silently, his teeth flashing in a rare grin. "It all depends on your point of view. You must learn to appreciate fine differences."

"To hell with fine differences. I'm interested in staying alive."

"Genna!" Mingus called out from ahead of them. "You should take pictures of me with the machete."

"Hold it over your head," she told him as she left Jorge's side and approached.

Mingus smiled for the camera and cocked his arm. Paulo and the Indios continued to work.

"That's it," she said under her breath, "this is what you want." She exhausted the rest of the chips in the cartridge while Mingus postured, the holocam whirring like some jungle insect as each image recorded its string of binary code.

℞

Dirt brown. White. Gray. Splotches of silver and red. This time the holo remains an abstraction even on closer examination. Whatever image has been recorded, it is blurred beyond any chance of recognition. Yet despite its lack of realism, the piece stands out as one of the most immediately striking in the exhibit. There is a sense of violent movement here, perhaps even violent death. One knows instantly...intuitively...that the bright streaks and splotches running through the cube like a random refrain are tracks of fresh blood.

∛

They heard the basso roar again, this time close at hand. Mingus once more pleaded to move faster. Moments later they broke through a particularly stubborn thicket and entered a clearing. Trees still towered about them, but the track of the old highway and the land around it were clear of brush.

Jorge called a halt. He sent Paulo and one of the Indios to scout ahead. Mingus threw down his machete and fumed. He paced back and forth along the perimeter of the road, fondling his rifle, looking up and down the trail. He was a pathetic man, Genna thought, but nonetheless dangerous. The strength of his obsession gave him a kind of stature. She had noticed how the Indios, generally impassive, often treated him with deference.

"Look!" Mingus shouted, startling them all.

He was pointing to the exposed root system of a towering ceiba, his outstretched arm trembling with excitement. "Wild roses...Therese's favorite flower. I know she must be nearby. I can feel it!"

Genna looked around. Low thorny vines with small white blossoms draped the roots of most of the trees in the area, and in some cases, had begun to twine up the trunks. Other than the trees, they were the only vegetation that survived here.

Overhead the sky had begun to darken. A low churn of distant thunder rumbled past them. By the time the scouts returned, large, widely spaced droplets splattered against the forest floor and dripped from the overhanging foliage, a slow tepid rain that did little to ease the heat of the day. Jorge conferred with Paulo and the Indios, and then announced something that disturbed Genna.

"The jungle is rarely this open. And now my men tell me it's clear of brush for at least a kilometer ahead."

"Then it should be easy to spread out and sweep the area," Mingus said.

"Paulo claims this is cleared land," Jorge continued. "And kept that way."

Genna snorted. "That's absurd. No one lives out here."

"Precisely, señorita."

"Precisely what?" Mingus looked wild-eyed and confused.

"Precisely why we'll stick together. And move cautiously."

"I'm not waiting," Mingus announced.

Jorge squinted through the falling droplets, which gave him a predatory look of shadow and power that intrigued Genna. "It is your choice, señor. I implore the others to remain."

Mingus looked to the Indios and Paulo, who stood behind Jorge and made no move to join him. Finally he fixed his gaze on Genna.

"What about it? Do your services end here, too?"

Genna shook her head, not in denial but disgust. "You know I won't carry a gun."

Mingus smirked and patted his weapon, then stalked off along the road, which now rose up into higher country. Rain threw darkening streaks onto the grooved trunks about them. While Jorge set two men on guard and with the others began to pitch camp, Genna watched the tan of Mingus' khaki outline shrink to a blob ahead. She gasped when it disappeared, followed by a loud shriek. A single shot rang out.

"Chinga!" Jorge shouted.

He motioned his men forward. They broke into a slow run, controlled by Jorge's sense of order. Genna followed. The terrain swept up a slight ridge and across a dry stream bed, where the carcass of a tapir boiled with huge flies and gold scavenger butterflies. They moved laterally around the base of a wide gargantua tree and came upon Mingus wrestling with a silver bird, its feathers flashing like mirrors. The siren eagle clawed at his face and pecked his bald head as he struggled to beat it off, while its mate—a smaller female—circled to nip and bite at his legs.

Genna was too stunned to reach for her camera. Jorge cut the smaller bird in two with a burst from his machine pistol. Mingus' other attacker rose straight up over a low limb of the gargantua. While his men shot blindly through the leaves, Jorge rolled on the ground until he was out of the limb's shadow. He fired in a wide arc, and a bird the size of a man plummeted to the forest floor next to Genna.

The eagle had lost a wing, yet still lived. It pecked at roots and the ground with its beak, pushing itself away from her as best it could. The shattered stub of its exposed wing bone traced an uneven line in the dirt. Genna at last had the holocam in place. Bloodied silver feathers writhed in the rain-splotched tableau of her viewfinder. Her hands trembled as she took the shot. For a lengthening moment afterwards, she stared straight into one of the bird's sad yellow eyes, and it seemed as if the creature were about to speak to her, to reveal some secret of the forest or of life itself. Then Paulo stepped forward and broke the eagle's neck with a vicious swing of his rifle butt.

Genna covered her mouth and turned to where Mingus lay.

"I saw her," he moaned, trying to rise, "I saw Therese! She's alive!"

"Stay still," Genna told him as she knelt by his side. "Don't move. You're just getting dirt in your wounds."

Mingus continued to fight the bird in his mind, his arms thrashing wildly about his head, and Genna had to sling her camera over one shoulder and pin him down. After a brief arching of his back, he gave out and lay spent on a tangle of dead branches and crushed leaves. His neck and head were lacerated, bleeding profusely, too messy to determine the extent of the damage. A gash on one leg opened to the pearly gristle of ligament. More scratches covered his hands and arms. His blood speckled Genna's camouflage shirt and pants, already dampened by the rain, and she immediately wished she could change.

"All right," Jorge said, "We'll camp here and tend to Señor Jahns. Paulo, set up the sonics to stop any sucker bugs attracted by the blood. And get those dead birds outside the perimeter."

As Paulo and the Indios moved into action, Jorge came to Genna's side. Mingus' eyelids fluttered and he tried to speak, but all that came out was a frothy moan.

"He says he saw his wife?" Jorge asked.

Genna nodded.

"But where?" One arm sweeping to take in the empty woods.

At that instant—Jorge's arm in mid-swing—lightning struck the clearing, blindingly bright, momentarily blanching all color from the scene. The thunder was simultaneous and deafening, rocking the ground beneath their feet. The rain fell more rapidly. Genna blinked as an after image of the flash overlaid her vision and pulsed across her retina like a black and white hallucination. The silhouette of a woman's torso, a stylized face in stark chiaroscuro, a face she had never seen in the flesh yet knew by heart. Genna realized that Jorge was kneeling by her side and they were holding one another like frightened children. His body beneath her hands felt softer than it looked. Several moments passed before either of them gave any sign of letting go.

☙

The frame is cast as a dodecahedron, elongated and tapering at one end, so that the structure as a whole might be likened to that of a cubist egg. Within its faceted brilliance, either nature or the holographer is playing tricks with color.

A cascade of wild roses fills the sculpture, blooming with such abundance that the vines from which they sprout are barely visible. The petals of each and every flower are open to their fullest and glistening with water droplets. Not red petals. Not white or yellow. But petals of the palest emerald green.

؃

Rain continued through midday and into the afternoon. With Mingus bandaged and resting in his tent, rendered unconscious by the poison that tipped the eagles talons, Jorge joined Genna in hers.

They made love fiercely at first, with shared abandon, Genna's cries rising into the static of the rain. At the height of their desire, the Castilian cried out also, in Spanish, calling on a god he had long since abandoned, tears falling freely from his eyes to dapple her shoulders and breasts. As the storm abated, and their touches grew more lingering and ceased altogether, Genna felt drained rather than sated. Turning away from Jorge in the narrow bed, she drew up her knees and folded her arms across her chest.

Everything was awry in this jungle, she thought, even basic human emotions could not be trusted. She saw the rainforest as a kind of rogue holo artist, the distortions in its vision not only altering the natural world it surveyed, but the lives and minds—the souls, if she could trust such a concept—of all who crossed its boundaries. Mingus' obsession and false bravado were magnified to the point where a normally calculating personality was transformed to that of a reckless fool. Jorge's rigid military mask grew more rigid until it cracked, revealing the child within the man. And here she was, Genna Opall, whom friends and colleagues, even lovers, had considered conservative in the ways of the flesh, having surrendered herself to a man she barely knew. If they traveled farther into the forest, would their individual distortions continue to increase? Perhaps at frame center, she thought, each of them would confront a self they could never have imagined.

Jorge cupped her body from behind with his, stroking her hair, breaking in on her thoughts.

"Why do you take pictures?" he asked.

"They're not exactly...pictures," Genna answered after a moment.

Jorge laughed softly. "What are they then?"

"Just computerized images. Numbers really. When I get back to the studio I'll project them into matrices and then play with them."

"It's not like developing a photo, then?"

"In some ways. Only I have more control over how the picture takes shape."

"I have trouble imagining this."

"It's a new process using a silicon base that is sensitive to light. It takes two-dimensional pictures and projects solid shapes from them, something like the way crystals will grow in the right solution. The final structure is inherent in each crystal. A three-dimensional solid, actually a host of possible solids, is inherent in each two-dimensional image. I alter the structures as they develop, impose my own vision on them."

"Like the rainforest imposes its vision on all that grows within it."

"Yes, in some ways it's exactly like that."

"But that doesn't answer why. Why do you take holographs?"

"It's not an easy question," Genna answered. "Why does any artist create? In part, I want to capture life and preserve it, or at least my vision of life. I want to collect people and remember them."

"Oh? Am I just another in your collection, then?" Jorge teased, his hand slipping lower along her side and across her belly.

Although she felt both desire and need stirring within her, Genna took Jorge's wrist, gently but firmly, and lifted his hand away from her body.

After several seconds, without speaking, Jorge rolled away from her and stood. He dressed quickly and silently. Genna didn't turn to look, but she imagined the expression on his face. A bruised look of rejection, soon to be replaced by the stoic mask once again.

"Chinga!" Genna heard him exclaim for the second time that day, as he ducked out of the tent. She gathered the thin blanket around her and followed, turning back the flap to look.

It was cooler outside. Sunlight had broken through the clouds and the rain had become a rising mist, swirling back toward the sky in the wind that followed the storm. At the center of their camp, the three Indios sat crouched in a small circle, passing a burning pipe and mumbling fearfully to one another. The wild roses Mingus had noted earlier, clinging to the exposed roots of each tree, now grew up the trunks to the height of a man. Their white blossoms had more than doubled in size and were now tinged with green.

☙

Shot at close range and enlarged further, several dark wormlike creatures stand out upon a ground of blue. The blue exhibits a wrinkled and reflective texture, perhaps that of a thin plastic sheet. Aligned in the same direction, the creatures appear to be on the march. In this blow-up they are the size of cats or small dogs. Their heads and torsos are visible in great detail: segmented, wet black, covered with erect cilia, bloated as if they have just fed.

୪

Whether due to a misplaced sense of duty, or because they were all now tainted with the mania of Mingus' obsession, Jorge decided to make one more try at locating the humani. After showing Genna how to work the sonic projectors, he set out with his men in the late afternoon, carrying a remote phone. He explained that when they wanted to reenter the camp, he would call in for her to shut off the sonics.

"Stay put," he told her twice, once before leaving and again on the phone, a few minutes after the party had disappeared over the first rise.

Genna wandered the small confines of the camp. Since the lightning flash her visual sense seemed heightened and at the same time distracted. Calm as the clearing remained, she felt barraged by the images around her: the trunks with their vines of roses, the branches overhead and the clouds moving swiftly behind them, even the plastic of their tents as it snapped in the breeze—along with the images she had experienced throughout the day—the dying eagle, Mingus patting his rifle, the sharp silhouette of Jorge's shoulder blades as he moved above her. Together, these crowded in on her consciousness with a kind of leap-frog intensity so that no single impression survived for long.

She checked on Mingus several times. Except for the gash in his leg, his wounds were not severe. He was resting peacefully, with no apparent fever. Yet either some-

99

thing in the siren eagle's attack or another poison of the forest had infected his system. His ruddy complexion was much paler and the flesh around his eyes, wrists and ankles was noticeably olive in hue and beginning to swell.

Again she wandered the campsite, unable to concentrate, images past and present assaulting her consciousness. Although there were several holo possibilities at hand, she could not frame a picture in her mind. Her camera remained in its case. The sonics continued to repel whatever creatures might be wandering nearby. Except for the occasional cry of an unseen bird, she might have been alone in the forest.

The calm was shattered near sundown.

Jorge's voice, so breathless and hysterical she hardly knew it as his, came crackling over the receiver, telling her to shut down the field. Moments later Jorge and the Indio known as Mercao staggered in from the woods. Between them, they half dragged and half carried the limp body of Paulo.

"He's in a bad way," Jorge said, lowering Paulo's body to the ground. "We met with eagles, then suckers. They seemed to be working in unison against us!"

"Where are the others?" she gasped.

Jorge tore open his friend's shirt without answering.

A large silver insect clung to Paulo's chest, its legs and eye stalks writhing. Jorge wrenched it free and crushed it beneath his boot heel. Paulo lay still.

"My God!" whined Jorge, "he's dead, too!"

Genna pulled him to his feet and shook him. Jorge's cap was gone and his hair now wildly awry as hers. Damp blood oozed from a wound somewhere on his scalp, plastering several dark strands to his forehead. More blood, already dry, ran in parallel tracks along one cheek.

"Get hold of yourself," she said, her arms closing about his chest and squeezing tightly. "You're still alive!"

She could feel the pounding of his heart and his breath was heavy against her neck. He returned her embrace, yet there was no strength left in his arms. The Indio, squatting and rocking on his heels, had begun to chant.

"You're right," Jorge said after several seconds, in a voice more like his own. "It is the living who count."

He stepped back from her, coughing and nearly losing his balance. Genna helped him to the ground, leaning him back against the broad trunk of a gargantua. The green roses framed his drawn and wounded face. His eyelids began to close...and then snapped open.

"The sonics!" he exclaimed.

Genna reactivated the field and quickly returned to his side with the med kit from her tent. The Indio squatted nearby, motionless, his voice rising in an ululating wail, then sinking to a serpentine hiss punctuated by soft clicks. He was crushing small red seeds in his palm and daubing his face with the sticky residue. Genna tended to the gash in Jorge's scalp as best she could in the fading light. His eyes were closed but he was not asleep.

"We must bury Paulo," he told her. "The smell of death has to be covered as soon as possible."

Once his head was bandaged, drawing on some inner reserve of strength, Jorge rose to his feet. He shook the Indio from his trance and unfolded shovels from one of the packs; they both began to dig in the soft dirt. Genna lit their fire for the night, and then joined them.

"Make it wide," Jorge said. "More of us may soon die. No point in digging twice."

Genna gave Jorge a look of intense horror, but said nothing. Afterward, they ate dried beef and cold tortillas from their stores. Mercao, the surviving Indio, declined the food and sat at a distance from them, smoking his pipe. Mingus had still failed to stir. By the rays of a lantern, Genna could see that the greenish swelling had begun to spread up his cheeks and along his forearms. While Mercao took the first watch, Jorge joined Genna in her tent, not to make love, but so they could hold one another against the night.

"Tomorrow we will leave for the coast," he told her. "Nothing more but death awaits us here."

She slept restlessly, her mind filled with dreams unlike any of her own. She dreamt of Mingus' accordion of plastic photos, only it contained not pictures of Therese but of her and Jorge, of dead Paulo, of the Indios, and a score or more of other faces she did not recognize. Mingus removed them from their envelopes and shuffled them like cards, laying them out upon a table, picking them up and shuffling them again. Then Therese entered the dream, not the Therese of the photos but a woman transformed by the forest and somehow a part of it. Her flesh was green like her eyes, eyes that no longer suffered but were filled with an inhuman insolence. She was naked but for the vines of wild jade roses twining from between her legs to wind about her breasts, belly and thighs. She joined Mingus in his game and they passed the cards back and forth, laughing and whispering to one another like infatuated lovers. They placed bets with the piles of chips scattered before them, not poker chips but holochips, like the ones Genna used in her camera.

"The forest is a woman," Therese told Mingus, smiling mysteriously, one narrow green hand cupping the chips in the center of the table and sweeping them to her side. "The forest is a womb."

"You are the forest," he answered, smiling back at her, oblivious to his losses, his small eyes hard with lust.

Genna saw that the table on which they shuffled and passed the card-photos was the cleanly severed stump of a gargantua. From the exposed concentric circles of its old growth, a new growth sprouted: a pale, scruffy fungus that had already begun to adhere to the cards and cover the faces on them.

Near dawn Genna awoke, alone, disturbed by a painful itch. The blue plastic walls of the tent glowed intermittently as distant flashes of heat lightning illuminated the horizon. For a moment Genna thought she was still dreaming, for the dimly flickering walls seemed to be covered with writing. When she lit her lamp, she stifled a cry. Its feeble rays revealed tiny black maggots everywhere. Some had already dropped onto her bedroll and embedded bristles in her arms.

After she methodically extracted the barbs with a tweezers from the med kit and sprayed the small puncture wounds with antibiotic, Genna went to check on Mingus. His tent had also been invaded by maggots, but his cot was empty and the man was gone.

ဢ

In this larger-than-life portraiture the features of the face are grossly distorted, the flesh tattooed more intricately than that of a Maori mask. Cheeks and brows swollen. Eyes mere anthracite pebbles. Jowly wattles beneath the bulb of a chin. Nostrils broadened to bestial dimensions. Open mouth like a slash of mud.

Even at close range, the expression of such features is unreadable. Take a step or two back and they vanish beneath the colors that scar and adorn them. In patterns geometric and organic, brilliant hues splay across the surface of the flesh...or rather within its surface.

For on closer examination once again, it appears that this is not flesh at all. Its rough and variegated texture resembles that of a canvas thickly encrusted with translucent paint.

☙

"At first light we'll retrace our path to the Para," Jorge told Genna over their predawn cook fire, "and follow it downstream to the coast. Anything that's not essential, we leave behind."

"Not my camera," Genna told him.

Jorge shook his head and made a dismissive gesture.

"And what about Mingus?"

The Castilian looked to the woods beyond the perimeter of their camp. The trunks of the gargantuas receded into the near darkness in irregular columns. They stood like pillars, seeming massive and numerous enough to uphold the sky, their branches cloaked in shadow, their bark obscured by the clinging vines.

"There's nothing we can do." Jorge's eyes looked sunken and desolate. With their expedition in ruins he seemed completely demoralized, any semblance of military posture abandoned. "The bastard is on his own now."

The Indio maintained his distance from them, his face streaked with red dye from the seeds, his lips moving soundlessly. Although he continued to take Jorge's orders, since the death of his fellows Mercao more than ever ap-

104

peared to inhabit a world apart. He was no longer eating, but drawing on his pipe constantly. Pungent smoke from the native drug filled the clearing, and when Genna inadvertently inhaled a whiff, the rush of exultation that followed took her by surprise.

We shouldn't be retreating, she thought for a moment. We should advance farther into the forest. We should find Mingus, Therese, and the humani. She felt certain they were on the verge of an incredible discovery.

Then her mood plummeted in a wave of dizziness, leaving her shaken and confused.

They were loading their packs at Jorge's direction when Mingus returned from his night in the forest. Or at least the thing that Mingus had become. The man wore his transformation for all to see. He staggered into the clearing in the half light before dawn, looming larger than his usual bulk, with a gibbous hump weighting his shoulders, and legs that swelled through bursts in his pant seams. One arm dangled uselessly at his side while the other, outstretched and trembling, performed arcane, sweeping gestures, as if sensing the air before it like the antenna of a bee. He spoke to no one, nor took any notice of their presence. Instead, he wandered through the campsite, halting to stare at the embers of the fire pit, at his tent, the handles of the shovels standing in the mound of dirt near Paulo's grave; anything man-made warranted attention. He rarely looked up or apprised himself of his location, as if his steps were random and he was only able to focus on the objects immediately before him. Except for his right arm, which twitched with a life of its own, he moved like a patient newly awakened, rediscovering the world after a long and feverish dream.

"As if our problems weren't enough," Jorge said, nodding toward Mingus.

"Mercao can handle him," Genna suggested.

"Mercao will save his own skin first." Jorge rubbed his chin and scuffed one foot in the dust. "And I'm tempted to follow his example."

"But," Genna said with a pause, as she considered the implications of Jorge's comment with regard to her own safety, "he's recovered enough to walk. He looks almost strong."

"He can walk," Jorge agreed, "but is he ready to leave? Will he do what we tell him to do?"

Genna raised her holocam and moved toward the hulking figure. Mingus ignored her. He stared at one of the sonic projectors. His good arm danced and turned in the air above it as if he were performing a ritual exorcism, or composing sentences only he could read. His concentration was absolute. When Genna trained her camera on his face, she made a startling discovery.

Mingus' flesh was covered with the pinched and deformed fractal structures known as Julia sets. She had seen studies of them hanging in the galleries at Soho, captured in the static medium of glass panes. These complex shapes started at a central point around Mingus' eyes and spread in elliptical curves, like the arms of a spiral galaxy stretching out from its core of stars. Some made fuzzy vines, some paisley patterns, some webs of lace or dust clouds, some the ciliated structures visible on insect chitin under an electron microscope. And all were in constant motion and change.

Genna zoomed in while the latest pattern shrank to a circle, then a blob, then generated another fractal that grew and advanced in increasing levels of complication.

The design swirled out around Mingus' left eye with a seahorse tail, shading the lid and eye socket in a shimmering powder blue. If such a display were manifest on the skin of a man, she thought, then something elemental had infected him, something so central to his genetic makeup that it could alter the pigmentation in his cells.

But it wasn't pigment involved after all. It wasn't even skin. When Genna zoomed the lens in farther on Mingus, to the center of one swollen cheek, she detected a film, roughly textured, that mimicked and exaggerated the lines and pores of the epidermis. This ragged growth, which appeared to be a kind of fungus, possessed a cloudy sheen that captured all colors at once. When intently focused on, an individual patch might appear azure, orange, yellow or any shade, but only for a fraction of a second. Then a new wash of color would shift across it, riding the fractals like a wave, gaining intensity as it rose from within the shallow depths of its translucency. How the successive patterns and colors controlled this cycle and displayed themselves so effectively, Genna couldn't begin to guess. How Mingus managed to survive with his physiology so radically altered was a further mystery. She clicked a series of studies at different levels of magnification, and then let the camera dangle about her neck, baffled by the phenomenon.

There was little doubt that Jorge's surmise was correct. Mingus was no longer the same man who harassed his hirelings and attacked the forest with manic energy. He was passive and subdued, a captive of the vegetable integument that covered, she now realized, not only his face but his entire body, including some gauzy fluff that threaded and consumed patches of his khaki pants. Even if he were capable of communication, she doubted the man could be motivated to follow them in their retreat. He would have to be prodded. Or dragged.

A loud roar echoed through the jungle, both plaintive and menacing in its timbre. If this were truly the call of the humani, as Mingus claimed, the beasts were very near. As Genna raised the camera to catch any reaction from her subject, she sensed Jorge by her side. He placed one hand on her shoulder, his grip tightening.

"We must leave," he said fiercely.

A second roar sounded, and a breeze from nowhere swept the clearing. Shreds of the growth that webbed Mingus' clothes broke loose to ride the air like dandelion seeds.

Genna dodged back to avoid any contact with the swirling spores, crowding Jorge with her, yet even as her weight and posture shifted she kept her lens trained, cranking up the magnification to capture Mingus' face in full portraiture. She was operating at peak efficiency, moving like a dancer with the holocam as her balance point, each of her shots framed with an uncanny sense of timing and composition. She had experienced this kind of involvement before, this oneness with the creation at hand, while reshaping holographs in her studio, but never with such intensity, and never while working in the field. Even if this were a further dislocation of her personality, another spell the forest had cast, she accepted its enhancement of her talent and the heady rush that accompanied it without a second thought. Here was the real answer to Jorge's question about why she took holographs. This sense of timelessness...of durable lucidity ...that transcended the identity known as Genna Opall.

The bestial roars became an ill-timed chorus, and Genna watched in complete fascination as a new series of changes shifted across her viewfinder. The throaty calls about them were mirrored in the light show on Mingus' face. She clicked a shot as the intricate fractals gave way to bold abstractions that pulsed with fluid ease. A wave of luminous orange claimed the distorted visage before her, flowing like lava across a miniature landscape, obliterating all in its path. Genna wondered what the man's flesh must feel like, if each visual change also caused a corresponding change in texture. When she thought about touching Mingus, all she could imagine was the bizarre growth that covered his body crumbling beneath her fingers, infecting her own pores. She pictured herself enveloped in fungal scum as she staggered blindly into oblivion, the cries of the forest mirrored in the chaotic art across her face.

Rather than recoiling from the image, her racing mind extended its logic. That must be it. She understood at last. The patterns were not random or self-generated...they were a mirror. Not of the cries themselves, but of Mingus' response to them.

"Now!" Jorge shouted, wrenching the camera from her hands, causing her to lose her footing and stumble against him as the strap caught on the nape of her neck.

For the first time, Mingus seemed to notice them. He glanced up from the sonic projector and his good arm fell to his side.

"Mus fine Threesh," he said.

"What?" Genna asked.

Mingus worked his mouth open and shut to clear the elastic threads of mucus that stitched his lips. One large thread curled around his jaw and disappeared into his chin. The volcanic orange was fading from his features, replaced by colors pastel and cool, mostly green.

"Therese is here."

The man's eyes did not focus on Genna's, but stared at her mouth.

"You aren't well. We must get you back to civilization and a doctor. That's what's important now."

"With the natives at the front, we can push on."

"But Mingus, the Indios are..."

"The men can hack the growth while I watch for her, follow her signs. They're everywhere."

"The three of us are all that's left," Jorge said, "and we're leaving. You can either come with us or stay here and join the others."

Genna saw that Mercao had come to stand by Jorge's side, his eyes riveted on Mingus, the pipe dead in his hand. Again the breeze sprang up from nowhere. As more of the fluff from Mingus' clothes broke loose, Jorge and Genna shifted upwind, but the Indio held his ground. Several of the airborne spores lit on his hair and face. Scrofulous white like large scabs of dandruff, they stood out in sharp contrast to his darkness. Mercao made no attempt to brush them off. He continued to stare, mesmerized by the apparition before them.

"Signs everywhere," Mingus went on. He had not turned to them, but spoke to the spot where Genna had stood. "Just this morning I saw a tent flap unravel to writhing vines. The shovel handles are no longer wood. Oh, no...they are beetles in a tight formation, barely discernible, ready to deconstruct at any moment. And other things are no longer as they seem. The signs are there. She's taking over. She's—"

"Mingus, you're crazy," Jorge shouted. "Shut this stuff up!"

"Green roses are blooming everywhere."

"Mingus!"

Genna said, "I don't think he can hear you."

Another roar seemed to emanate from the very air about them.

Mingus cocked his head to one side. "Therese has sent her voice. She's speaking to us."

"You see, he responds to sound."

"No, Jorge, only certain sounds. His communication is one way."

"Therese!" Mingus yelled as he straightened his misshapen shoulders. His limp arm suddenly came to life, jerking in fits and starts like a marionette. He raised both hands, clasped with fingers intertwined, as if in supplication to the immense tangle of roses that now covered everything below fifteen meters surrounding their camp. Genna became aware of their fragrance for the first time, a dense floral pheromone, nearly sickening in its overpowering sweetness.

"Let's see if he'll respond to this," Jorge said.

Grabbing one of the shovels, he approached Mingus from the side and jabbed him with its spade.

The fabric of the man's shirt split as if it were rotted; a patch of the white growth beneath tore away. Mingus' actual flesh was revealed like a raw wound. Tiny beads of red swelled and ran into rivulets. The fungus was rooted in his veins and arteries, drawing its nutrients directly from his bloodstream. Before Genna could assimilate this horror, another was upon them. The spade of the shovel fell from the handle in Jorge's grip, and just as Mingus had predicted, the wooden handle disintegrated to countless scurrying black beetles.

The Castilian stumbled backward, beating the insects off his sleeves and trousers, cursing incomprehensibly. He called to Mercao for help, but the Indio stood motionless, rooted in place, the white flakes spreading across his face.

"Therese!" Mingus roared, oblivious to the assault and its aftermath. A fresh wave of color erupted across his forehead and flowed down his cheeks, the fractals forming and disintegrating with increasing rapidity. Other roars sounded from several directions at once, in response to his call.

Genna's heightened awareness had not deserted her. She perceived the clearing and the forest beyond with incredible clarity, each successive moment charged with significance. She could feel the breeze, now a steady wind, rocking the branches and rustling the leaves over their heads, wafting the scent of the roses through the camp. She could see the beetles, scattering in a widening circle from the spot where the spade of the shovel had fallen. Behind her to the east the rising sun cast long, oblique rays through the foliage to speckle the ground with dancing lozenges of light. To the west the sky was immersed in the deep blue remnants of night, a few stray stars and a silver moon fading from sight. She raised the holocam and pivoting full circle, without conscious thought, clicked off one shot after another. When she looked up from the frame of her viewfinder, beyond the field of the sonic projectors and into the lightening woods, she could make out several huge animals circling the rose thickets. They moved on all fours with a loping gait, their shaggy heads bent low, narrow snouts sniffing the ground before them. She knew at once that these were not the humani, at least not from the descriptions Mingus had given them.

"Maned wolves. Once the size of dogs," Jorge said in response to Genna's unasked question. He had returned to her side with the machine pistol gripped in bloodless hands. His tone was desperate. "As to why they're wearing roses..."

These Amazonian wolves stood tall and stout as bison, with high shoulders and necks ringed with a thick, rust-colored fur a shade or two darker than their body pelts. Their long ears pointed and twitched; their eyes flashed like coins minted in burning metal. Twining about their torsos, either freshly cut or rooted in their bodies as the fungus that claimed Mingus was rooted in his, were the same vines of wild roses that covered the trunks of the gargantuas. One beast directly downwind from Mingus dipped its black nose to sweep the earth, then raised it high, as if trying to sniff out a path around the compressed, high-pitched sound barrage that held it at bay. Genna flinched as the animal yawned. Its incisors were as long as her fingers, and wickedly serrated down each side.

Mingus grew increasingly agitated. Both of his arms began to writhe in the air, his entire body jerking and twisting with uncontrollable spasms. He turned awkwardly by fits and starts to face the woods, to stare directly at the wolf. The beast suddenly ceased its motion, as Mingus now did, and stared back. There appeared to be some silent message passing between man and animal, a voiceless simpatico.

"No!" Jorge screamed, as Mingus reached forward and shut off the sonics.

In the foreground, frame center, a wolf with the mane of a lion raises it snout and, presumably, roars. One red eye is visible. It shines with a light of its own, as if the skull of the beast were illuminated from within. It emotes a kind of feral energy that makes one uncomfortable to hold its gaze for long.

By its side stands the figure of a woman, draped from head to foot in vines and green roses, seductively poised with one leg and hip thrust forward. Or perhaps this is just the representation of a woman, a provocative topiary sculpture cut from leaves, from emerald thorns and petals. It is impossible to tell which. Uncertainty lies at the heart of its striking and somehow dangerous beauty.

Behind the two figures the woods lie in light-splotched shadow, clogged with a dark skein of intertwining growth. And further still...a patch of dusky sky...an oblate moon so pale and featureless it could be no more than a nub of polished bone.

⅓

The wolf trotted forward but made no move to attack. Several yards short of Mingus it let out a high piercing cry and sank back on its haunches, letting the tangle of vines and flowers that encircled its body slip to the ground. Or so it seemed. The tangle continued to uncoil as if possessed of its own energy. Vines stretched to the height of the wolf's shoulders and beyond, taking on the form of a tall and statuesque figure. Definition increased and the figure itself materialized—a face, bare limbs, its body clothed in vines like some dryad spirit. Then the flowers and vines alone took precedence once more. Then the figure again. Genna rolled off half a dozen shots before this flickering juxtaposition ceased and the vision before them solidified to a singular image.

A woman—for the revealing lacework of vines left no doubt as to gender—stood before them with hands planted firmly against her hips, thighs spread, one leg slightly forward. Although the individual features of her countenance resembled those of Therese, this was in no way the long-suffering wife portrayed in Mingus' photos. Nor was it likely the creature was even human. A thatch of russet hair, dark as the fur of the wolves and of similar texture, fell to her waist. Her flesh was a pale green, its complexion smooth and unblemished as a sapling stripped of bark. Wide-set eyes showed a deeper sea green, nearly iridescent, and as she surveyed each of them in turn, her passing glance was cool and mercurial as the sea. Yet more than the sum of her physical attributes, her inhuman beauty, the creature before them projected a poise and surety that reached charismatic proportions. Although Genna had never wanted a woman before, she was inexplicably drawn to this woman. She felt an attraction both carnal and sublime that overshadowed her sexual identity. And she forced herself to look away.

Mercao and Jorge seemed to have no trouble staring.

For the first time since fastening on Mingus, the Indio had shifted his gaze, though he remained as fixated as before. Jorge scratched the stubble on his chin as he scanned the woman several times, head to foot. He leveled the machine pistol at her chest.

"Therese?" he said.

"The gun will do you no good."

The voice was haunting and persuasive. From the edge of her vision, Genna saw Jorge begin to lower the weapon to his side. She found herself wondering if the woman spoke out loud to them or merely seeded their thoughts, draining their wills with a kind of hypnotic charm. Was the figure before them a Therese transformed by her sojourn in the rainforest, or some incalculable spirit of the forest that now wore a semblance of her shape? Genna's sense of clarity was gone, illusion and reality a swift jumble in her mind. Did she stand by Jorge's side in the clearing or was she already like Mingus, wandering at random through the trees, lost in fantasies of her own making? Would the entire landscape soon decompose to scurrying black beetles? Were the roses even green?

Genna looked back to Therese, and again strange thoughts welled up within her. The woman grasped the wolf by its mane, pointing the animal toward them like a weapon. Wind ruffled the mane and caused Therese's hair to billow about her face and bare shoulders. Morning light fell through the trees to illuminate the forest behind the pair, etching every leaf and flower with exquisite precision. The composition was perfectly balanced, each of its elements inevitably in place. Yet even if the scene before her were real, Genna knew that no static photo, even a holographic one, could capture its intensity. She made no move to reach for her camera. Instead she felt the need to rush to Therese's side, to assure her they meant her no harm. She wanted to hold this woman and suffer the scratches of her thorny garments, to rip the vines aside and press her mouth to the pale green flesh.

"I have come to take Ming."

With this mention of his name, presumably the very diminutive by which his Therese had called him, Mingus moaned and fell to his knees. Thick sighs escaped the man's lips as he began to edge forward, his body crouched low to the ground. He moved hesitantly, as a beast in heat might approach its prospective mate, irresistibly drawn yet wary of the object of its lust.

"He's in no shape to follow you," Genna heard herself say.

"He will be fine soon. The transition can sometimes be harsh."

"No damn transition here," Jorge said. "The man is dying. That fungus is eating him alive." He again raised the machine pistol, but his movement lacked intent.

"Death always precedes rebirth."

Mingus had reached Therese's side. Still on his knees, he embraced her thighs, burying his face in the trailing vines. Genna saw that small tendrils were already sprouting along his own back. Therese accepted his attentions but took no notice of him. She gazed directly at Genna, and the unabashed invitation in the woman's eyes forced Genna to look away as before, in shame and confusion.

"You're welcome to join us. All of you."

"Join you?" Jorge said pointlessly. "What do you mean? We're already here." His voice was breathless, a thin shade of its former self.

Next to succumb was Mercao. Perhaps because of Therese's proximity, the patches of fungi had already merged to cover his features, their shifting colors mingling with the red of his face paint. The Indio stumbled forward, prostrating himself in the dirt at Therese's feet, his body trembling with fear or excitement.

"Yes," Therese laughed, a sound unnerving in its girlish simplicity. "I have known many of your brothers."

Clearly they were not the first travelers through the forest to encounter this creature that manifested itself as Therese Jahns. How many others, Genna wondered, had been induced to join her in this vegetable transmutation and whatever bizarre existence it entailed? Did the forest abound with beings once human but no longer, vines and leaves and flowers that had been living flesh?

Jorge, visibly aroused, fell to one knee, either to conceal his condition or because he was no longer capable of standing. He made the sign of the cross like a reflex, and then dug his fists into the dirt. Genna didn't understand how, in his weakened and demoralized state, he had managed to resist the seductive power that flowed from Therese this long. Yet as she helplessly met the woman's eyes once more, it became clear that Jorge was incidental to Therese. There was no longer any doubt that Therese was speaking within her mind, speaking directly to her. Not with words, but the message came clear. Their desire was mutual. She wanted Genna to join her, not only sexually, for that was but a small part of what she offered. Therese spoke not only to her sensual needs, but to her aspirations. She was more than some dryad spirit spawned by the constant mutations of the forest. Rather the reverse was true. Therese was a creator of the forest, or at least of this area she now inhabited. And she was inviting Genna to join her in that creation...to live out the ultimate dream of artistic megalomania as she helped to shape and reshape the fauna and flora all about them like some immense living holograph.

Yet even as this vision claimed her conscious mind and Genna took a faltering step forward, she discovered a part of herself that resisted and remained separate, not denying the force of the emotions that raged through her and left her trembling, but observing and interpreting them, claiming them as a source for further expression even as they transpired. It was the artist within her, that very part of herself that Therese sought to possess. And it was that same self that now understood that although there was great beauty here, perhaps even greater passion, the spirit that fashioned and ruled this world was ruled in turn only by endless curiosity, by arbitrary and childish whims that left it indifferent to whatever suffering or joy it engendered.

Genna knelt by Jorge's side and taking one of his clenched fists in both of her hands, she pried his fingers apart and pressed their palms together. And when she felt his grip tightening on hers, and she could sense the growing warmth in their touch, she spoke back from within her mind to this spirit who called her. She silently screamed her denial with all the strength of her human soul.

Therese shrugged as only a goddess could, supremely indifferent to her loss. There would always be others.

She turned away, both Mingus and Mercao, or whatever vegetal monstrosities they had become, rising and turning with her. The maned wolf turned too, but not before it gave both Genna and Jorge one final glance, its eyes flaming with a knowledge that belied its form. It was a look filled with disdain and disregard, as if it too, like the mistress it obeyed, were a superior creature.

Genna and Jorge watched Therese and her wards retreat through the trees. The other wolves that had circled the campsite followed in their wake. As the strange entourage grew smaller in the distance and vanished over a rise, the wind that swept the forest suddenly died. A preternatural silence, undisturbed by the call of bird or beast, settled upon the clearing.

All about them, the roses began to change color.

“”

For the pièce de résistance of the exhibit, Opall has cast a massive sexahedron. The sculpture stands five meters high by ten by eight. Within its oversized dimensions one sees a forest landscape that encompasses earth, trees and sky.

The light that floods the scene fingers down in beams that are broken by the profuse growth. The trunks of the trees are strangled with roses, many a virgin white, some yellow, many pink, others a blood red. And though this seems to be the same clearing as depicted in some of the earlier holographs, not a single rose is tinged with green.

As one begins to circle the massive block, the illusion of a simple landscape is dispelled. In the branches above the roses, disembodied faces begin to appear and disappear, flickering in and out with every few steps, face after face, as different in color—red, yellow, brown, white—as the roses below, and more varied in expression. Some seem calm and at peace, their eyes closed as if in sleep. Others reflect the blissful glow of intoxication. Others are staring blankly. Still others seem to be howling in rage against the leafy prison that encloses them. Hovering above this assemblage, at the lower limits of the sky, seen only from a certain angle, but then another, and another, a larger face appears, a single enigmatic countenance that reigns like a ghostly eminence, nearly invisible among the branches for its flesh is the same shade as the leaves.

MYCELIUM VALLEY
Boston

In an isolated valley
of the Mutant Rain Forest,
eternally occluded
by low-hanging clouds
that constantly spill rain

onto the land below,
vegetation is smothered,
trees are being pulled
down to the earth,
towering ceibas and

year-old saplings,
not by the weight of water
but by immense coverlets
of fruiting mycelium.
The fungi are everywhere:

gray, blue, aquamarine,
flaming orange networks
and iridescent outcroppings.
The fungi are everywhere,
an expressionist collage

filling the drenched air
with their spores
and a stifling plague
of eruptions heralding
no life but their own.

SEDUCED BY THE MUTANT RAIN FOREST
Boston/Frazier

Roving archaeologists
and other human scavengers
mine this transilient Yucatan,
unearthing ruins long since dead
and cities dead for only months,
slashing at the colossal growths,
cursing at the dense swamplands,
searching out some rare find
to make their name or fortune.

At El Mirador I compete
with them for jadeite masks,
for broken knives and shields,
for shards of eighth century pottery,
"treasures" that rot within our packs,
that prove to be nothing more
than clever imitations
generated by the metastases
of chameleon tubers.

Burdened by my failure
to resurrect the shifting past,
buoyed by recurrent dreams,
of a return to home and renown,
I endure the monsoon season
along the Rio de la Sombrio
as its rain-drenched belly darkens
and eels its emerald way
to the blank heart of the forest.

Bedded in a champa built

from leaves and wattled reeds,
I marvel at milkwhite iguanas
and welcome a new symbiosis
with miniature kinkajous
who pick the lice from my hair.
I feel the values of my own past
surface like blood-soaked thorns,
infections held too long within.

One night in a rocky clearing
near a glistening oxbow lake,
a tribe of migratory looters,
intoxicated by the microspores
of an addictive pavonine moss,
act out a ritual as violent
as the land they traverse
to initiate a stranger
into their barbarous clan.

Hoisted on a barbed liana
and patterned by my own blood,
I envision quetzals and serpent
maidens with flayed hearts.
I cry out in the sibilant tongue
of some lost warrior caste,
hissing at the wheeling stars,
calling on the waxing moon
to cleanse my tarnished self
with the harsh alkaline intensity
of its bone-piercing light.

THE PAVONINE ADDICT SPEAKS
Frazier

"Hanging gardens of ragged, lacy orchids...whole towering forests of their heads...their mouths open like women gasping in ecstasy...these breathless echoes mingle with the sad echoes of swamp dwellers...the mating rituals peak...within the hive the queen is devoured and from her blood the sisters are brood-readied...within the rivers the razor-cats grapple in territorial battle...their teeth like needles and their wormy beards tipped with powerful stingers...within my venal tributaries the singing rises and falls...the moon hangs like an overripe fruit...slashed by the wings of transparent bats...fat with blood...they seek the lapping pool of my soul...the quiet place where ancient maidens bathe...their tiny throats speak in languages too shrill to hear...their cacophony sets the orchids ashiver...a translation I understand...tongues of silver...I speak back to the milk-drenched odors they expire...the night babbles around me...I breathe it...it breathes me...breathe me..."

A GOURMAND OF THE MUTANT RAIN FOREST
Boston

His jaded palate
is startled and refreshed
by a wealth of flavors
so subtle and provocative
that frissons of delight
shudder up and down
his meaty back,
by pungent aromatics
so utterly unique
he once again discovers
the first unbounded passion
of his sensual decay.

From a penthouse suite
safe within the Seattle dome,
he expends his fortune
on delicacies more
bizarre and illicit
than a cannibal's feast.
He bribes customs officials
and employs unsavory sorts
so that he might savor
the fruits and meats
of a furious ecology,
so that his taste buds
might embark upon
vicarious exploration
of far rivers and climes
he would never dare
to visit in the flesh.

Even the pains which
rack his portly belly
do not lessen his desire
for spiny bone-white guavas
seasoned with banana moss.
The rash of radiation welts
which erupts upon his chest,
his throat and forearms,
does not delay his hunt
for the perfect table red
to complement the spicy
roasted sweetbreads
of the anaconda sloth.

He is discovered
one morning slumped
before his laden table,
nearly unrecognizable
in the stench of his decay.
The slender stalks
of saffron fungi
which sprout
from all his orifices
have reduced him
to an ectomorph
and scoured
the plates before him
till they shine,
yet have left
a ghastly rictus
of gluttony revered
upon his face.

RIO DOS MUTANTES
Frazier

Drift diving the altered Amazon
starts with a siren's sibilant song.

Is it pressure on my inner ear
messing with my concentration?

These aural imaginings must arise
from my tanks, from a bad mix of nitrox.

Who tampered with my gear?
Too late to nix this flood season swim...

My fins drag up a dusky particulate,
a blackboard for the existence of seraphim

that can attract razortails to a blood fest,
or dartworms that hook your heart like bait.

Every diver studies such grim mutations
& knows the layouts of many river beds.

But which way exits this drowned forest?
Or which instead will hasten my demise?

My stick & glide feels so impure.
My handholds slip from my grip.

Above me barbed mosses train
down from branches a maze to navigate.

Immense pink dolphins wink golden eyes.
Is there meaning in their gaze?

& a swelling balloon leech supplies
its road map of fluoresced veins.

Which is the proper course...I'm unsure?
I see specters sway on silt stalks.

Each weedy mouth talks my name
& bids me down inviting currents to rest

on glades of writhing gorgonheads,
between stinging red lines of devil's tears.

So let me defame these grotesque fears.
So let me invoke each sacred river force.

My data recorder can source my route
and divine where this end reboots.

Oh, let me whisper incantate
& confess my fate to the black box.

MUTANT ILLUMINATION
Boston

Rebel saints and stray pariahs,
   clever con artists and stalwart desperadoes,
     mad adventurers and rogue fanatics,
devotees of all that is *outré* and fantastic...

embrace the transfigurations of this spacious borderland,
   this unexpected frontier where individual imaginations
        can chance freedom and death beyond
            the hermetic wisdom of dome-dweller cant,
beyond the futureless ghetto entrapment
of the unshielded urban sprawl...

where it is rumored that in a valley yet to be mapped,
somewhere in the vast interior of this organic labyrinth,
   light, the very *spiritus lux* incarnate,
     roams the treetop canopy silently
        from branch to intertwining branch...

spilling a liquid radiance from the cups of flowers,
   rifling the hidden plumage of exotic birds,
     peeling an ebon sheen
        from the chitinous backs of arboreal beetles...

gathering diverse shades and blending unseen colors
   to cast an illumination so archly pure
          in its dusk light clarity
   that it fills the leaves with a rarefied translucence
for miles in every direction...

so potent in its distillation
   you must smell and taste and savor

its foxfire nectar with every intake of breath,
    so vital in the implications
of its visionary promise
    that tears will rule your cheeks...

and you will know with a certainty akin to madness
    that all the unnamed appetites of your questing soul
    could soon be sated...

STIGMATA
Frazier

Prelude

And everywhere I look upon the Sphinx's skin,
*   memories spin; they form from the formless...*

At the lost horizons of New New Guinea, in the forgotten
        highlands of Papua,
the Koranga river tumbles wild as the riprap that fans into
        her valley
from the sheerest mountain sides. She spills not far from
        the coast, not far
from a world still trying to adjust, yet quite distant in
        such a riotous terrain
where fresh growth reaches out and strangles you with its
        verdant grip.
Along her banks sits a lone outpost of civilization, a
        desperate foothold
of subsistence, and pig farmers, and the miners who crush
        gravel for its gold.

There I drowned—in cheap liquor—my memories of a
        woman's brown eyes.
There I bared my torment over the unscalable limitations
        of love.
And there I sought Wutai, a man who owned the town
        and had a reputation
for knowing every person, every crazy tale that passed
        along the Koranga.
In this case, a rumor that a powerful faith had sprung up
        in the jungle depths,

a back-to-the-roots religion of animism and rebirth in
    nature, a truth
that might free me from the remorseless grip of what
    obsessed my spirit.
Wutai and I were destined to bargain, but I knew little
    of what I bargained for.

     1.

In the Mutant Rain Forest where everything dreams, yet
    nothing sleeps,
        in its replenished interior that is the shade of the soul,
            where ancient fires still rage and sputter dead,
            I sometimes see my own death shapeshift before me,
                                a flashing vision

On the night I found Wutai, with monkey calls
    keening through the treetops,
with a waxing moon that sparked silver fire in the clouds
    about Mount Kaindi,
and after swelling my courage with shots of Wutai's rum,
    I sat on the steps
of his canteen, talking with him, waiting for a guide
    Wutai expected soon.
A seasoned explorer who Wutai would hire out to me for
    a price, and who
he guaranteed would lead me to Bulolo—the mad bishop
    of this faith I sought.
I watched the incandescent pupils of headlights scythe
    through the streets
lined with candy-colored huts, with flaking attempts at
    cheer.
The vehicles turned off; always false hopes. I twitched as I

cursed.
Tired of sitting and drinking, bone sore from waiting on
     bare façades
in the abandoned outback of No Place. Waiting for my
     rapture, my savior.
I knew something had better happen, and sooner than
     the next drink.

Inside, the band blasted through another loud, lurching
     song of joy.
Thatched roofs lifted, the walls of the building seemed to
     sway
seductive as hips on their block pilings. I leaned against
     the steel rail,
stretched my legs along the length of the step, and turned
     my face to the door.
Strung over the dance floor, Christmas lights flickered
     like heat wasps as
the six-piece group segued to a staccato, reggae-like
     medley.
Weathered men in stiff chaps brushed their electricity
     against giggling Lolitas.
A bar girl named Mani poured Wutai and me a round of
     black coffee.
Wutai, sallow-faced, with eyes hollow from smoking coca
     paste, slurped his.
I held mine up, hoping to divine my future from its
     calligraphies of steam.
Mani lingered at the threshold and stared at me with a
     pouty expression,
a smoky emotion that all women here bore like a cross
     against their bosom,
a sign that a man must interpret before offering up his

heart to them.
Even in this regenerative paradise, the soul suffered its
    cloisterage.

Music stopped in an abrupt decay of drums and guitars. A
    brown out.
A woman in a blue top stepped from the shadows and
    confusion with a cigarette,
dismissed the girl, and got a light off me with a quick
    penetrating look.
When she disappeared again into the steamy mass inside,
    I followed her
compact movements with an appreciation born from
    years of insomnia.
"You like that one, eh?" asked Wutai. "She's half native."
"Just watching for the sport," I said, half in truth.
    "Spectator sport."
"Good, Mani wants to fuck you. It's okay. She's clean, and
    she likes it quick."
He gestured as if tossing off lines to an advertisement.
    "And she has spirit!"
"Spirit is good," I said. "But I like it slow, and with
    conversation. I like mystery."
I stopped talking then. The emptiness had pooled inside
    me, pressing to get out.

    2.

I sometimes see my own death shapeshift before me,
                    a flashing vision
        of scales patterned in a lambent bronze,
in a stream of rays that runs liquid as the days.

The generator kicked in, and the band leader stepped to a

big microphone.
Before he could sing, the woman in blue stumbled out—
    shoved past us.
Three surly men corralled her near a red flatbed truck
    with boarded sides.
The woman sank to her knees in the mud of the parking
    lot. She swore.
One rancher stood over her, spoke in pidgin that clucked
    from his throat.
She laughed like a madwoman, saying something about
    paying for drinks.
The man raised his fists and shook them. His words were
    unintelligible growl.
She laughed again, taunting him in a voice that I heard as
    a toucan's squall.
The man hit her, quick and deliberate with flat of his
    palm.
She bellowed. She wasn't an animal that he could buy and
    sell.
She moved to stand up, but he hit her again with a
    sweeping backhand.
His friends tried to subdue him, but he was incensed now.
Drunk enough to rage with mean spirits, to do damage. I
    stepped to the ground.
"It's not your fight," Wutai warned me with a grip on my
    shoulder.
I shrugged him off. Everything had become a struggle for
    me.
I slid across the wet earth, wove through puddles with a
    sinuous gait,
materialized between the rancher and the girl as he raised
    his fist like a hammer.
"You savvy, this stop," I said. The man dropped his hand

to his waist.
A flash of metal arced toward me, lashed out, catching my
	wrist,
and I followed each scintilla of reflected light, each grain
	off the blade,
as I swung an elbow up under the man's forearm and
	drove outward.
With the knife deflected, I jabbed hard to his midsection.
The rancher staggered back, a groan exhaling from his
	lips.
I connected with a solid boot toe that raised his manhood
	six inches,
sent him sprawling like meat against the side of another
	vehicle.
He collapsed as might a seaport village under monsoon
	rains.
I started to shake, my legs barely holding me as I walked
	away.
The girl ran off, cupping her bruised cheek and cursing
	along the street
until I could no longer hear her over the drunken croon
	of the band leader.

I sat beside Wutai, inspected the long gash down the back
	of my hand.
Cut to the bone and gristle, but little blood—as if the
	wound grew there,
and the incision had only served to unfold its clean pink
	secrets.
Wutai removed a hat banded in grime and wiped the
	sweat from his puffy face,
blotting it from his creased jowls with a handkerchief
	mildewed by blue spots.

"Was it worth it, Mister? You didn't even get the girl."
His irises looked dark as sapphires where the lights
    caught on their surfaces.
"And now you must worry about contamination in such a
    wound.
Out here, the spores can root through your marrow, seize
    your blood."
Wutai spoke with such sang-froid that it sent a chill
    spiking down my back.
Hadn't he warned me that such a problem might occur?
I felt that he had indeed known the outcome of the fight.
That he prefigured every event that occurred in this god
    forsaken hole,
every round of Saturday night seduction and duplicity
    and murder,
and every pincer of the rainforest's campaign against
    man's occupancy.
"Now, what about Mani?" he said. His eyes turned
    depthless, indecipherable.
I shook my head. "I'm through with sex. I'm here for
    salvation."
"But my guide will pass through. Tomorrow, maybe.
    Maybe the next day.
Your payment will not be lost. And Mani is here tonight!"
I ignored him, discovering that another gash opened
    along my forearm.
I accepted pain. Began to stutter. To itch where more cuts
    burned
like an unrequited passion. I told myself that I deserved
    them.
Wounds of guilt. Of yearning. Of my true caring severed
    by a woman's fear.

3.

It is a Sphinx that lifts the world upon its back and growls.
Its veins are roadmaps that lead nowhere,
its breath a cipher

Wutai said, "Sometimes men aren't what they seem. But
    they are still men."
He looked puzzled as he spoke, then smiled as he pointed
    toward the dark
shapeless canopy engulfing the town. "You know, the
    trees are weak.
They have mutated very shallow roots in the jungle, even
    the giant kinky.
Despite their girth, a cable and two jeeps can pull them
    over.
Ah, a man's resolve is no different. A man needs love to
    carry on."
My wounded hand palsied. I caught it in my other,
    squeezed it hard.
The pain spread tongues of warmth through me,
    replacing my destitution.
I wanted to say, "A man can survive on his pain, if he
    makes that choice."

Wutai patted me on the shoulder with an air of
    patronage.
"You look pale, Mister. Perhaps we should go inside to the
    rum?"
As we stood, I heard a strangled cry from the brush that
    bordered the canteen.
A tribesman ran breathless into the lot, tripping and

landing face down.
He thrashed the mud with his arms, staggered up, and
    ran straight
into Wutai, who caught him by a mop of stringy hair,
now caked into muddy dreadlocks across his painted
    chest and arms.
A ragged hole remained where the man's nose had been.
    His ears were lace.
The muscles on his face danced as if bees swarmed just
    beneath their surface.
The very top of his skull supported a fungal mass that
    glistened in the moonlight.
Wutai said, "This is not the guide to Bulolo. But he is
    certainly of their church.
Perhaps the forest has brought this one to you as an
    omen."
Wutai sat again with a look of apprehension veining the
    slack of his face.
His voice sounded more precise, more educated than he'd
    first let on.
"Sit again, Mister. We will comfort this man. And Wutai
    will talk."

"Far at the depths of old Papua, where the river builds her
    white anger,
Bulolo keeps a church carved from the heartwood of a
    massive kinky tree.
And around it, living roofless in the canopy, his followers
    congregate."
(At the mention of Bulolo, the native slumped forward
    and lay at my feet.
He breathed in deep, gasping rhythms while Wutai
    continued his story.)

"The novices of Bulolo do much worse than *kai kai*, than
  eating men.
They feast on the forest: edible barks, foxfire fungi, the
  rodent-like things.
They drink such nectars that infect them with unnamed
  contagion,
or with hallucinatory trances that are the dreamtime of
  the forest.
They seek to commune with the virulent growth that
  seeds their land.
And in doing so, their fallen spirits may rejoin the
  perfection of nature,
may participate in the rebirth of the world through
  change and regeneration."
(At this, the native's back began to heave, the skin
  bunching in cabled knots.
I watched the musculature writhe and seemingly align
  anew.)
"And this takes its toll on any zealot," Wutai said. "For
  they are all zealous.
Their skin droops in wattles. Their hair blooms or falls
  out forever.
The bacteria swarm in colonies through their pores,
  annexing the flesh.
They become something more than a man, and
  something much less.
They seek oneness and rebirth, but I am unsure what they
  truly find."

The native's skin began to alter in hue before me, to a dull
  yellow-red,
the color of an open wound suppurating with pus and
  blood.

From this base—nutrient rich—fine rhizomes sprouted
    and tendrilled,
sooty black as the branching air passages in a rock miner's
    lungs.
They matted to a mycelium knotted with buttons of tiny
    orange fruit.
They mounded on him, formed a topography of the
    mutant landscape
crawling with faceless stick figures, seething spore-
    bearers.
These things embraced then fought; mated and—it
    appeared—died.
Finally, they fused into a winged beast, a panther with the
    skin of a boa
and the wings of a great bird, and this image birthed a
    bronze-colored cub
as the man moaned in something resembling a wind-
    borne chant.
Thus, Wutai's monologue was made corporeal before my
    eyes.

    4.

*Its inscrutable eyes spin mandalas that drift and blue
                        shift in toward Armageddon.*

Within minutes the native had healed, a process in which
    the growths shrank,
withdrew from his back, and the man stood on both feet
    in good vigor and
shook Wutai's hand. He then staggered on to some other
    rendezvous, enslaved,
perhaps, by a need to convert the world through his

obeisant displays.
I sat with Wutai in silence and watched the monkeys
     dance on the shoreline,
acting out a primal play of lust conquering, of lust
     spurning.
What riddle had the rainforest placed before me in the
     body of that man?
And Wutai, was he a facilitator in this riddle? Or a
     separate challenge?
My skin crawled with emotion, perhaps a foreshadowing.
I realized that my bargain with Wutai was not what it had
     first appeared,
that his offer of a guide was an offer of himself, of his
     instruction,
and for him, my pilgrimage here was to Wutai, not to the
     bishop or to the wilds.
Bulolo's trail guide was no more than a figment of Wutai's
     dementia.
No man explored these jungles for long; no man returned
     unmodified.
Certainly, no man would come to lead me physically to
     my own healing.
I had not sought salvation so much as I'd sought escape.
I had not sought truth so much as I'd sought an elaborate
     lie.
Wutai sensed this and offered a woman and some down-
     home wisdom.

I walked down to the river's edge, skipped stones into its
     cauldron pools.
The mist gathered, wet my eyes, and for a moment my
     resolve broke.
I knew then I must find the center of the rainforest for

myself,
accept its changes on me as I had accepted the wounds of
     a shattered love,
of a woman I'd left far behind in the cubicled cities of
     America,
of a woman who had known my heart but feared the
     power of her own,
who feared the thin illusion that my life was staid and
     stable,
feared rejection and its loneliness where none was
     possible from me,
feared the intensity I had leavened into friendship.
I must accept that we could've loved, could have reached
     unscalable heights,
yet we'd feared—we *both* feared—the raw, exposing
     power of that act.
These were inescapable insights. Yet it seemed I could
     escape them.
And in the mutable heart of darkness, I would act out
     their stigmata,
a broken man laboring at every moment to live with my
     truth,
my flesh opening for each new spore to implant
the solace of its corrupting visions.

Coda

*In the Mutant Rain Forest where everything dreams, yet
     nothing sleeps,
     in its replenished interior that is the shade of the soul,
       where ancient fires still rage and sputter dead,
     I sometimes see my own death shapeshift before me,
                              a flashing vision*

of scales patterned in a lambent bronze,
in a stream of rays that runs liquid as the days.
It is a Sphinx that lifts the world upon its back and growls.
Its veins are roadmaps that lead nowhere,
its breath a cipher,
its inscrutable eyes spin mandalas that drift and blue
shift in toward Armageddon.
And everywhere I look upon the Sphinx's skin,
memories spin; they form from the formless...

THE TALE WITHIN

Robert Frazier

In the hot season of a hot year, on a pilgrimage through the superverdant interior of the Mutant Rain Forest that spans from old Belize to the swamps flooding Panama City, I retraced the route of my father's expedition in a series of rattletrap buses. Drivers plowed their vehicles through black bottomless mud holes, and on the roads linking the high passes, harpy grandmothers would lock my arm in a death grip as we snaked down hairpin turns whose shoulders fell away hundreds of meters to the cloud forest below. It seemed plausible that my father had been swallowed by this nightmare. Lost, yes, but not killed. He epitomized the adage that says every sailor must be prepared to take the wheel of the ship. I had considered it on this trip several times.

Worn by lack of sleep and constant delays, I left such a bus one afternoon while it was stopped at a border crossing from Honduragua into Costa Rica, and I followed a vine-choked alley toward a bar overlooking the Rio San Juan. Another passenger walked with me: shorter than I, rotund, dressed in khakis, with salt-and-pepper hair and a pronounced facial tic. When we reached the patio that overlooked the ochre waters of the river, he insisted on ordering us an iced pot of maté.

Just what my spirits needed. A Brazil-sized jolt of caffeine.

"Going far?" the man asked with an Irish accent as buoyant as my mother's.

"I'm not sure where I'm going," I said.

We both looked away to a thick log that floated by us in the water, and the back of a glassy iguana that rode upon it. Its transparent flesh resembled a map of red and blue roads. In a seamless motion, the log rolled, swallowed the glassy iguana whole, then flipped its branch-like tail and dove into the current, no doubt to surface upriver and begin another search for a tasty passenger.

"Ah," he said. The man seemed restless, stirred in his depths by an invisible hand. "You're here for the jungle. A photographer, right?"

He gestured at the camera bags I had carried with my suitcase from the bus.

I said, "I do some of that."

"Thought so," he smiled. "I'm a guide working out of Managua. McMurphy's my name."

No emotion showed in his milky jade eyes. He relied on facial muscles.

"Oh, I'm not soliciting. I specialize in canopy work, and I'm dead set against taking out another *tourista*."

I made a weak effort to uphold my end of the conversation. I kept hearing my mother, seeing my mother in his mannerisms. The breathy sonorities, the twitch, the deep need to tell everyone her circumstances. This man might someday fall silent as she had, succumb to a powerful grief or to some secret that already ate at him from within.

I said, "Kind of narrows your options."

His cheek spasmed. He shook his head as he spoke. "After what happened a year ago, I'm sticking with biologists."

"Last year?"

"Nothing you'd believe for long, I dare say."

"Please continue," I assured him. "I've been distracted."

I reached out and gave his hand a vigorous shake. His sweaty grip felt tenuous, as if his arm might come off at the shoulder.

"I'm Rob," I said. "Rob Breslin."

"Ian," he said. He looked wistful for a moment, like a schoolboy gathering his thoughts before a speech.

"Okay. It began just about this way, you know. A sleepy town. A long stopover. A story to be told. Only it wasn't my story, really.

"This kid was looking for his roots. He told me he'd been abandoned on the doorstep of an American mission in Mexico City, and now wanted to find his family. He backed this with a roll of money that smelled faintly of drugs and fast cars and city life. He claimed he'd been the offspring of a native woman and a white traveler who'd retreated into the wild.

"Now, his skin didn't have the right look, if you know what I mean. Instead of a rusty bronze, he was pale, with black hair matting his chest and arms, everywhere actually. His nose had been broken, flattened to his face, and his eyes showed yellow as wheat straw. He had a spiky mustache, too." The man rubbed the hair above his own lip. "Mestizos don't grow much face hair, you see."

I said, "I'll remember that."

"Anyway, we set out to cross the steep eastern slopes of the Miravalles volcano. He felt certain that his family lived in the wilds above the waterfalls there, at a commune in tree houses. They worshipped the jungles as a *paradiso*. He'd hired me for checking the treetops, and we did just that. He was bloody loony, I soon realized, but it was too late to turn back. All that first day he mumbled stuff about jaguar men and the need to stay hidden."

Jaguar men! Those words pierced my chest like a poison barb. My father had come to these parts to trace such a rumor, based on specious accounts that a missionary on the Isla de Ometepe had harbored a small group of mutated cats who walked erect. His theory held that they were shaved, disguised in holy cloth, and sent south with two monks across Lake Nicaragua, to where the Mutant Rain Forest was impenetrable.

I didn't mention this to McMurphy. Nobody gave my father's expedition credence back then; I didn't judge McMurphy to be any different.

I said, "What about these Jaguar men?"

"I know this won't make sense, but bear with me."

He freshened our cups with more maté and ice.

"We'd been traveling for two and a half days, and the kid had survived a touch of dysentery, the hallucinogenic stings of lime ants, and an encounter with a very nasty bat. Barely twenty, but he had guts. On the morning of the third day, after a hard rain pelted our hammocks, we heard a cry. A haunting cry. I assured him it was only a Kong sloth, you know, but he insisted that we descend in our harnesses and start off toward where we'd heard the call. Within three hours we were pumping our ascenders into the low sucker branches of a peculiar gargantua tree."

"You can't summit a gargantua manually," I noted, setting my feet up on a battered chair. "Even the saplings rival the Empire State Building."

"So you know something of this forest." McMurphy's eyes widened and he plucked at his goatee. His expression always seemed in flux. "That is good. Very good.

"Anyway, when he stated that morning that he was serious about attaining the crown, an impossibility as you say, I suggested we rig a few emergency motors to our gear. We wired up these rigs with battery packs, and soon climbed in relative peace, tugging at the ropes with our arms and elevating through a mist illumined to violet by the rays of sunset. A swarm of eagle-sized butterflies passed below us. I glimpsed the Miravalles volcano smoking peacefully above us. You couldn't fault him for choosing a beautiful climb.

"I didn't sense that something was amiss—truly amiss—until the second afternoon in that tree, when we'd threaded up through the first big branches. I had to recoil the ropes and fire launchers for yet another leg of the climb. Here the bark appeared devoid of bromeliads and anaconda vines, say nothing of epiphytes. I'd never seen a tree so clean. I noted this, but the boy showed no alarm. By the time we'd reached the underbellies of the huge main branches of the lower half—thick as box cars they were!—and had stopped to fire the ropes yet another time, I also noted how uncluttered the main limbs were. As if some creature of the forest had deliberately pruned its millions of small branches and twigs just to strengthen the larger ones. It certainly made things safer for us, you see, but..."

"I know," I said, growing eager to hear the end of his story. "The gargantua grows so rapidly that its small limbs are too weak to hold a man."

"Correct," he said.

I brushed a bee from my sleeve into my palm. Its thorax looked as if a human skull was painted on it.

"So you also know that everything grows parasites here. And worthless branchlets below the leafy crest. Yet, as I said, this gargantua had been gleaned. In such a state, the crown might indeed have been reachable with enough food and our battery packs, as yet unused.

"The boy saw this and grew more agitated, and he started up before I'd hooked my harness and gear into the new run of lines. Switching on his motor, he built a lead, and he increased it with reckless tugs of the ropes that jerked him ahead faster. I watched as his figure diminished above me.

"I later found him on a high limb where the ropes ended. He sat cross-legged, paralyzed by what he'd discovered."

McMurphy paused to refill his cup.

"Go on. I'm in suspense."

McMurphy smiled. "Ah, that is what makes this welltold!"

I frowned. "He found what he was looking for?"

"Yes. Or so I imagine now.

"Before us stretched a small village of leafy huts built upon platforms of branches, and between them ran rope bridges made from the interweaving of vines. On a manmade canopy about them, large yellow bromeliads flourished in ordered rows, each with pineapple-like fruit at their center.

"The kid let out a cry like I'd heard that morning, only this time the haunting note seemed twisted by a sad need, an emotion so pent up that it had mutated like the jungle into something, well, tragic. It was as if..."

I said, "All right, all right. What happened?"

McMurphy shrugged. "Suddenly, I fell away from the sight."

"Your rope broke?"

"No. My harness let loose, tripped by a creature that had worked its way up under me. I zipped down at an amazing rate, managing to jam the mechanism just before my rope ended. The rope stretched and broke, then I slammed hard into rough bark—the feel of it is the last thing I remember. Next I found myself in a hospital with two busted legs and a cracked ribcage. I'd be dead if not for the orchid gatherer who found me. He dug me from a dense pile of leaves at the base of the tree. Before the blood mites drained me."

Downriver, our bus blurted its horn.

"End of story?" I said as I paid the waiter.

"Very much so. I never heard if the kid made it out. And I've never gone back. Though I might someday, just to prove I saw, well, what I saw. I might if I had the right reason to go back."

As we hurried toward the bus, McMurphy fell silent and I sensed a reluctance in him to speak further. I myself felt numb, unable to digest his story or even make a comprehensible whole of its parts. We sat together, but I dozed while he stared ahead into the setting sun.

When I awoke it must have been well past midnight. The bus had stopped in another town, and then wouldn't start. I stumbled out into the humid night to find a room.

Three girls from a hot pillow joint, their faces thick with garish make-up, helped the male travelers with their bags under a lone streetlight. I saw McMurphy shrug off their advances and head toward a hostel down the street. I followed at a distance and took a room in the back over the alley, only to wake before sunrise, overwhelmed by the smell of sewer wastes and a longing that coursed over and over through my heart like the deep insistent songs of sap locusts.

One clear dream memory of my mother's mouth wavered in my mind's eye. I heard her voice calling me.

With a fuss and a small bribe to the proprietor of the hostel, I managed to raise McMurphy. It looked as if he had slept upright in a chair, for neither the bed nor his clothing were rumpled.

"What's this about?" he said.

He squinted into my face as the sleepy cook brought us two mugs of weak coffee on a tray. McMurphy kneaded his hands, and we moved to a pair of ladder-back seats in the vestibule. Neon toucans flitted from bush to bush outside, their bioluminous bills making loopy streaks through the shadows. I wondered if these were messages. A ghostly foretelling, perhaps, of the success of my journey.

"Speak, Breslin! You must have disturbed me for a reason."

"I have a theory," I said.

His frown turned to a smile. "Ah. By way of trying to hire me?"

The steam from our drinks swirled in punctuation about our heads.

"You need reasons for your work, you say?" I cleared my throat. "What if I told you that the boy you left in the forest was half jaguar." I paused until his eyebrows raised in anticipation.

"Ah," he said. "You are still dreaming."

"Not at all."

"Well," he said as he stood abruptly. "I wish I were. You have wasted my time. I am not interested in this mockery of my tale."

"But…"

"I am sorry I began this."

He left the hostel abruptly, and I did not see him again until I made my way to the bus station two hours later. I confronted him where he stood by the ticket window.

"Ah! What a surprise. It's Breslin."

I nodded. "I believe your indignation is a ruse. You left out an important part of your tale."

"True," said McMurphy. "But neither were you forthcoming."

"Fair enough. That boy you guided into the forest was probably my half brother. I am searching for him."

"The resemblance did not escape me," McMurphy said. "But your face is not his. A different mother, perhaps? Yes. But you're not here just to find your brother, are you?"

"My father as well."

"He lived here? A *Notre Americano*?"

"Yes. He returned once with Paolo, when I was a baby, so that my mother could raise us together. Paolo lied to you about the mission steps and the orphanage. He lied to my mother about his reasons for seeking out my father in the jungle. She died waiting for my brother and my father to come home."

"Fair enough," said McMurphy. "What else would you know?"

I said, "You saw them. Didn't you?"

"Yes. They were stooped, long-limbed people who tended the fruits around their camp, and they had wrinkled skin, flattened noses, clawed fingers, and glittering eyes. I watched one man shave the dark body hair of another on the porch of the closest hut."

"They were cats?"

The color drained, no, shifted in McMurphy's face.

"That is possible. One of them stealthily got the drop on me in the harness. And knew what to do."

"Will you go back?"

"No."

"No matter my offer?"

"No matter."

An awkward silence engulfed us.

A large woman with a pale fungal growth engulfing one ear announced that the bus was finally repaired, and we boarded immediately. McMurphy and I settled in our original seats, distant by several rows, for the long ride into the molten core of another day in the hot season. By twilight, I was sleeping like a baby. The bus felt like a furnace.

Actually, it was a furnace.

I was jolted alert as the bus slipped off the shoulder of the road on the top of a burning ridge top, and it crashed on its side. Then the bus caught fire as the passengers and I poured like ants through the upturned windows into the surrounding darkness.

People were weeping and shouting. There was a bloody veil over the face of the driver, and most everyone looked disoriented. My senses hummed with adrenaline.

All at once the entire countryside seemed to be in flames. Smoke swirled about me on all sides. I pointed my nose into the wind and tried to sniff my way to freedom, probing for pockets of fresher air on the ridge. I growled directions to the others as they groped about in fear, but only McMurphy settled in beside me as I charged ahead toward a break in the smoke.

I veered around a clump of heavy brush that crackled with fire; the light formed a halo against the darkening sky. Passing the charred body of a deer, we hopped across an outcropping of rock so hot that it penetrated the soles of our shoes, then shot down a sharp incline. Broomsage smoldered, singeing my legs. Between columns of smoke that seemed to twist toward the moon, reaching to engulf it, I spotted lights in the valley directly below.

It was there I sensed the bind we were in.

We could not turn back against the inferno, placing our survival on chance or luck. Yet if we swept toward the bottom of the ridge, toward the lights, we would no doubt reach a cliff, and that was chancy. We might not see the edge in time. The choice felt impossible to make, though that mattered less with each fifty yards we crossed. The fire and smoke turned us downhill, and I could not fight the pull of gravity.

We plunged through brambles that seemed untouched by the fire, and ran parallel to the valley lights, but a wall of flame leapt at us and forced us even lower on the hillside. We moved north again, only to meet a slip where the earth had been softened by constant rains. The slip created an impassable gap, its bottom thick with mud, and about twenty yards farther down, the slip had collapsed into a full slide that left a ragged edge where it had dropped to the plain below. At the very top of the slip, flames licked through the weeds.

I hesitated; McMurphy seemed to wait for my decision. High on the bluff, the gouts of smoke still looked too thick to trust. And skirting below the slip meant chancing the very edge of the drop-off.

I edged down into the slip. McMurphy followed.

He held his footing in the soupy mix, motioning me to cross the gap as quickly as possible, yet I lingered inside, making sure that no passengers had followed us and become mired. That became a mistake in judgment. The land under the mud was clay, and my footing gave way and I landed on my ass heading downhill. I dug in my heels and kept my legs stiff, but they began to lose strength, so I thrashed with all fours, flipping belly-down to stop my momentum with my stomach. Another mistake. Now I could not regain my feet. Gravity sucked me to the very edge of the precipice, where I seemed to hang in suspension for a slice of eternity, clawing for a foothold. I pitched forward and saw dark treetops rise rapidly toward me.

The stars spun in streaks above me.

The night air rushed across my mud-soaked clothes.

Twisting to right myself, I slammed into water, front first. I kicked and stroked myself to the edge of a shallow pool, choking on weeds and snorting liquid from my nostrils. The shore felt heavenly under me. I collapsed upon it, lost consciousness...

And awoke moments later in a few inches of water, my head cradled in McMurphy's lap. All the adrenaline had drained from my body and my muscles hurt terribly.

"This is pavonine," McMurphy said as he fed me a sweet fruit that rapidly invigorated me. "It will reorient you."

When I shifted my gaze from his expressionless face, I was unprepared for what I saw.

The pool I had landed in was about an acre and perfectly round, a rare occurrence outside of the glacial terrain up north. The shoreline had recently receded several feet, leaving a perfect carpet ring of blood-colored grasses and transparent ferns, brightened by the tiny flowers of blue toadflax. There was a thin inner ring of very shallow dark water—where I lay—showing a few sprigs of knotty weeds. Save for the intrusive tip of a mudslide, the rest of the pond's surface appeared matted with the pads of a table-sized water lily—an olive-green plane dotted by pure white flower heads that opened to a moon that, surprisingly, blasted through the smoke-threaded sky like a searchlight down a well. A couple lemon-feathered birds buzzed inches above this in a chaotic holding pattern. Winking electric blue darning needles flitted from foothold to foothold. Close in my field of vision, a tiny frog stretched its tongue to impossible lengths for gnats, while further out, water beetles the size of cobblestones gave the pond's surface the look of boiling coffee as they rose between the lilies to capture an envelope of air with their back legs.

Then a great filmy bubble of swamp gas lifted from the center of the pond. At its center was a knot of fire, and its surface was figured with swirling iridescent hues, a Rorschach of color like the static of an early morning holovision, a shifting pattern in which you could see things, see images that moved and gestured and beck-

oned to you in ways that made your soul ache with longing.

My breath caught in my throat, perhaps from a reaction of awe at where I'd found myself, but just as much
from a sense of reluctance, a feeling that I should make as
small a disturbance as possible in this tableau of raw, un-
diluted beauty.

The bubble drifted our way. The sounds of the night
intensified. And the effect of the pavonine fruit wormed
deep into my brain stem. I saw McMurphy in a chimerical
light. Or else the light of truth, for I had seen something
like this happen to an ordinary garden tool in some village along the bus route, a spade whose handle dissolved
into threads of maggots.

A violent facial spasm sent a ripple up one side of his
head.

With a sense of urgency in my voice, I said, "I have no
brother."

McMurphy said, "And I have guided no one but yourself. This...this is all yours."

His flesh sloughed down his cheekbones. One eye
rolled from its socket and uncurled. It scurried down his
neck, a ganglion-like mass on dendritic feet. The eye
socket collapsed, his skull caved, and his entire body
slumped. Pieces broke into smaller pieces, no longer dif-
ferentiated, and then McMurphy dissolved into small
motes, into a rising cloud of tiny winged insects that began to circle a larger and larger path around me.

When the gas bubble from the center of the pool
burst, showering a thousand fiery beads over the lilies,
these insects lost their flight pattern and settled everywhere, melting into the grasses and bushes and water lilies and the fabric of my clothes.

McMurphy was gone, if you could say he was ever there.

He had been a vestige of the forest, a single cell in its vast green brain trust, and, as if I were that iguana on the log in the Rio San Juan, I had been carried in the drift, steered by McMurphy's influences, and finally swallowed up by the forest wilderness. It was up to me to emerge Jonah-like from the belly. Up to me to find my way alive to Paolo and my father.

What happened, how I survived, that is another story. It does not belong here. But there was an incident at the edge of the lily pool, just as I started out on my own, which will always stick with me as a defining moment for that passage.

I was gaining my feet, wavering a bit unsteadily, to say the least, when my hand and arm crossed my line of sight with the moon. The light seemed to pierce me. I remember how insubstantial, how like the iguana's meat my arm appeared. I thought I saw the muscles swarming and re-forming under the red caul of my palm. Following a purpose of their own. Agitated like bees on fire.

A chill swept through me.

Thankfully it passed, my vision cleared, and the night—such as it was in a place like this—felt normal again. I was weary of it all. I let out a sob of relief and hobbled off toward civilization out there ahead of me; while in their beds, unmindful of things of horrible dimension or the irrevocable import that might underpin the very fabric of their lives, the rest of the continent snored or coupled furiously or themselves drifted in a weary state, trapped in sleeplessness as if it were an amber sap that welled up from their souls.

SUMMER IN THE WORLD OF TWO SEASONS
Frazier

Those of the Stamen

In the jungle of mutable tulips,
massive stems thrust
above the storied cloud banks
and hold their crimson blooms
like acre-wide dish antennae
listening to the heavens.
Signals from the absolute
gather against their petals.
Dark secrets whistle
across their columned stamen
with the updrafts of storm fronts.
At dusk their pollen falls like gold
cotton upon the foothills below,
where the People of the Stamen
gather it for their shaman to digest
and divine the coming harvests
in a babble of red visions.

WINTER IN THE WORLD OF TWO SEASONS
Frazier

Those of the Fruit

With each snow fall on the mutant oaks,
buoyed by dreams of light,
the Yggdrasil acorn lifts high
like a mothership above the fjords.
Its cap hinges open to a nest
lined with eggs the color of icy water.
The People of the Fruit believe
that each speckle on those shells
encodes all knowledge:
a Rorschach of color
like the mysterious static
on their ancient television screens;
a shifting pattern in which they
see things, see images
that move and gesture and
beckon to them in ways
that make their souls ache.

RETURN TO THE MUTANT RAIN FOREST
Boston/Frazier

Years later we come back to find the fauna and flora
more alien than ever, the landscape unrecognizable,
the course of rivers altered, small opalescent lakes
springing up where before there was only underbrush,
as if the land itself has somehow changed to keep pace
with the metaprotean life forms which now inhabit it.

Here magnetism proves as variable as other phenomena.
Our compass needle shifts constantly and at random,
and we must fix direction by the stars and sun alone.
Above our heads the canopy writhes in undiscovered life:
tiny albino lemurs flit silently from branch to branch,
tenuous as arboreal ghosts in the leaf purple shadow.

Here time seems as meaningless as our abstracted data.
The days stretch before us in soft bands of verdigris,
in hours marked by slanting white shafts of illumination.
At our feet we watch warily for the tripvines of arrowroot,
while beetles and multipedes of every possible perversion
boil about us, reclaiming their dead with voracious zeal.

By the light of irradiated biota the night proliferates:
a roving carpet of scavenger fungi seeks out each kill
to drape and consume the carcass in an iridescent shroud.
A carnivorous mushroom spore roots on my forearm
and Tomaz must dig deeply beneath the flesh to excise
the wrinkled neon growth that has sprouted in minutes.

We have returned to the Mutant Rain Forest to trace
rumors spread by the natives who fish the white water,

to embark on a reconnaissance into adaptation and myth.
Where are the toucans, Genna wonders, once we explain
the cries which fill the darkness as those of panthers,
mating in heat, nearly articulate in their complexity.

Tomaz chews stale tortillas, pounds roots for breakfast,
and relates a tale of the Parakana who ruled this land.
One morning the Chief's wife, aglow, bronzed and naked
in the eddies of a rocky pool, succumbed to an attack
both brutal and sublime, which left her body inscribed
with scars confirming the bestial origins of her lover.

At term, the massive woman was said to have borne a child
covered with the finest gossamer caul of ebon blue hair.
The fiery vertical slits of its eyes enraged the Chief.
After he murdered the boy, a great cat screamed for weeks
and stalked about their tribal home, driving them north.
His story over, Tomaz leads our way into the damp jungle.

From base camp south we hack one trail after another
until we encounter impenetrable walls of a sinewy fiber,
lianas as thick and indestructible as titanium cables,
twining back on themselves in a solid Gordian sheath,
feeding on their own past growth; while further south,
slender silver trees rise like pylons into the clouds.

From our campo each day we hack useless trail after trail,
until we come upon the pathways that others have forged
and maintained, sinuous and waist high, winding inward
to still further corrupt recesses of genetic abandon:
here we discover a transfigured ceiba, its rugged bark
incised with the fresh runes of a primitive ideography.

Genna calls a halt in our passage to load her minicam.
She circles about the tree, shrugging off our protests.
As we feared, her careless movement triggers a tripvine,
but instead of a hail of deadly spines we are bombarded
by balled leaves exploding into dust—marking us with
luminous ejecta and a third eye on Genna's forehead.

Souza dies that night, limbs locked in rigid fibrogenesis.
A panther cries; Tomaz wants us to regroup at our campo.
Genna decides she has been chosen, scarified for passage.
She notches her own trail to some paradise born of dream
hallucination, but stumbles back, wounded and half mad,
the minicam lost, a disk gripped in whitened knuckles.

From base camp north we flail at the miraculous regrowth
which walls off our retreat to the airstrip by the river.
The ghost lemurs now spin about our heads, they mock us
with a chorus as feverish and compulsive as our thoughts.
We move relentlessly forward, as one, the final scenes
of Genna's disk flickering over and over in our brains.

In the depths of the Mutant Rain Forest where the water
falls each afternoon in a light filtered to vermilion,
a feline stone idol stands against the opaque foliage.
On the screen of the monitor it rises up from nowhere,
upon its hind legs, both taller and thicker than a man.
See how the cellular accretion has distended its skull,

how the naturally sleek architecture of the countenance
has evolved into a distorted and angular grotesquerie,
how the taloned forepaws now possess opposable digits.
In the humid caves and tunnels carved from living vines,
where leprous anacondas coil, a virulent faith calls us.
A sudden species fashions godhood in its own apotheosis.

A MISSIONARY OF THE MUTANT RAIN FOREST
Boston

In nomine Patris et Filii et Felidae Sancti

Cassock torn, rorshached by blood and sweat,
a detailed gold crucifix with broken chain
clutched so fiercely in one skeletal fist
that an intaglio of the thrice-nailed Jesus
imprints like a scar in the hollow of his palm,
he trods through patches of light and shadow
cast by vast vegetal eruptions he cannot name
except to christen them infernal or sublime.
Having penetrated farther into the wilderness

than any of his far less stalwart brethren,
all of whom have fled to the coast or died,
his aquiline features are increasingly set
in a rigorous mask of beatific masochism,
he is sustained by the fervor of a faith
more maniacal than the landscape he tracks.
The creatures of the forest do not harm him,
in awe of the madness inherent in his quest.
Swarming clouds of carnivorous red-jackets

shun the taste of his pale fevered flesh.
Or it may be his sermons that protect him,
leaden tracts rehearsed till letter perfect
in the sanctum of some distant spartan cell,
now raged and chanted through the awful glens,
against the scattered shards of unthatched sky,
embellished by a rising hallucinatory passion,
peppered with the mucous rattle of his breath.

On a morning born from nightmares he awakens,

no memory in his mind of how he came to sleep;
the congregation he has sought is all about him,
a flock of clever felines who walk upon two feet.
With the scraps of human tongue they've gathered,
they listen to his tales of the sacrificial son.
Here *his* faith is heresy, *his* form abomination,
he whets their appetites with his talk of blood.
As their paws and claws defrock him, pry the gold
from his hands, strip away his sacerdotal shreds,

his dreams take flight beyond a martyr's death.
He envisions the pomp of his future consecration,
in the Holy City, a host of hosannas sung on high,
yet the fate he soon discovers is far from divine.
Bound by mutant skins, stained with mutant dyes,
he becomes a penitent before a graven shrine,
novitiate and servant to a pagan panther priest.
For visionary madness is familiar to their kind,
and they only devour the ones they cannot teach.

In the ghetto of Caracas you can see him every day,
an excommunicant, a derelict, a holy man some claim,
a strangely-tattooed apparition both hirsute and gray,
who preaches the imminence of a feline Second Coming
and sees the reborn Saviour as a bestial incarnation,
complete with taloned forepaws and the eyes of a cat.

A TRADER ON THE BORDER OF THE MUTANT RAIN FOREST

Bruce Boston

From my mobile station on the shifting border of the Mutant Rain Forest, I watch them come from the Northern Domes, from the slums and ghettos and the failed farms of the Wastelands, the lost ones eager to surrender to the Forest's compulsions and the ones who tremble as if they are harboring a fear they must conquer. Then there are the religious ones, fanatics who come in groups. They think they are going to convert the creatures once-human who survive beyond the border, most of them already animal or vegetable in inclination and form. They think they are going to convince them to worship Jesus or Allah or Joseph Smith. Or the latest holovangelist.

I sell them satellite links that offer up-to-the-minute maps and weather forecasts for their implants and devices. How do I know if such maps and forecasts are accurate? I suspect the most accurate are far from reality. How can topographical maps on a holographic screen, shapes and lines and dots of color, even in three dimensions, portray the reality of crossing that same terrain? The searing climb of steep hills with muscles aching in calves and thighs, or the descent into valleys so deep and thick with growth you are plunged into a shadow world that your lanterns can't penetrate. And you have to guard your life every step of the way.

Yet the visitors buy them, and contribute to my subsistence on this lip of coastal land the Mutant Rain Forest has yet to claim. All such voyagers into the chaotic green of the Forest are fools by my count.

♋

There is still trade from the interior even in this savage land. I peddle native charms and potions as protection from the dangers one may encounter in the Mutant Rain Forest. I sell sachets from native plants, some of them extinct by now, for that happens swiftly in the world east of my station. Such talismans claim many things—to repel predatory animals and plants, to deconstruct the illusions of the shape shifters that mimic your friends and loved ones, who inhabit your mind with shadow images from the unconscious, or perhaps they are billed as an antidote to counter the deadly bite of red jacket wasps that can infest the spinal column with their larvae and make their victims dance to ghastly rhythms as if they were marionettes before they are devoured from within. The larvae gradually emerge as adult wasps from the human husk that remains, taking flight from ears, mouth, nose and empty eye sockets as they mature.

Do the jujus I sell work? I don't promise anything. You would have to ask those who have tried them. I have never believed in such nonsense myself. Nor have I ever chosen to visit the perverted terrain that lies beyond my trailer to test their efficacy. All that I know is secondhand and that is enough for now. Sometimes more than enough. I have heard tales of horrible deaths and trans-formations within that world I will not repeat and that I don't even like to think about.

I do not sell weapons. Archer was the one to go to for that. That faded blue trailer just opposite, five hundred yards on the other side of the clearing, the one aslant on two flat tires with the door canted open, that was Arch-er's. Last I saw of him was one night at the cantina. We used to get together some nights to talk philosophy and women and just about anything. Archer was a good friend. Not that many in a lifetime.

That last night he was drunk and talking crazy, about how we must surrender to the Forest, how the Forest held the true destiny of the human species. Next morning he was gone. It didn't take long for his trailer to be gutted by looters. There are no laws here to prevent such things.

ᘓ

From my station on the shifting borders of the Mutant Rain Forest I watch the fools return from their adventure, the ones who do. I sell them trinkets and souvenirs of their time here. Bizarre animal hides and skins, both fake and real, holographs and videos of Forest scenes they never experienced. The trade is always better when they first arrive. Most are too stunned in one way or another when they return, too self-absorbed to take any interest in souvenirs.

Some look shattered, as if the bedrock of their soul has been sledged by a hammer of the gods. Others seem to glow with religious fervor, many of the same ones who came to preach and convert now burn with the fever of a new faith. They have suffered and embraced revelations they must assimilate to continue with their lives.

There are others who have shut down all emotions. They wear a coat of body armor and their faces are expressionless. They are denying the changes that have been wrought upon them. Changes that wait in their brain's recesses and the marrow of their bones. Some will deny them forever, always in conflict. Others will come back to the Forest and make it their home.

And what of those who do not return from their adventure? Dead or changelings, so I have been told.

∛

As the Forest grows closer, as this lip of coastal land grows thinner and smaller, I know that my time will eventually come. Though I have never entered the Forest, I have lived too close to it for too long. Just like Archer.

Now I discover my thoughts returning more and more often to the Forest, and I am increasingly aware of the changes it has wrought upon me. The veins in my wrists, once blue, are now a greenish shade. There is a new surety and grace in my movements, a sense of balance that was lacking before. My vision and sense of smell seem more acute, as if the Forest is preparing me to survive within its borders. And I know that once the Forest claims the little land left to us, I too will become a fool like the others who have vanished into its depths.

So I wait until the time is ripe before I embark into those opaque walls of green entanglement, of death and transformation.

Though I have heard rumors of human tribes that still survive there, who have somehow made peace with the

Forest and live in harmony with it. Perhaps I will find one of those to join. Who knows? Perhaps I'll even find Archer.

PHANTOM LIMB

Frazier

Lost in the jungle wars
Against encroachment
His leg an empty space
Defined only by memory

Like a wild-hearted bird
Trained with sweet seed
The mutant forest repays him
Colonizes life back into limb

Reddish casting scarabs
Build bone from chitin
Their bug brethren form
Sinews of elastic wax

Flesh made of wingless bees
A skin of interlocking mites
In this way he strides home
On the rebirth of his sole

THE REACH OF THE MUTANT RAIN FOREST
Boston

The emerald infestations stretch their tendrils
through sand and loam. Expelled from volcanic

vents in the impermeable interior of the forest,
they rise as fertile ash upon the world wind.

They flow with ocean currents and their high
flying particles stream through the stratosphere.

Microscopic flakes settle in the Mariana Trench
and dust the cold white peaks of the Himalayas.

They penetrate concrete, steel and the meat of
flesh. The planet becomes a plague zone that

thrashes and thrills in the verdant fever of
its disease. Rich in bravura, pervasive in the

claim they make on the world, the manifestations
of the Mutant Rain Forest insinuate their claws

and tentacles into civilization's end, to inhabit
our lives and bestialize our lovers and friends.

CHILDREN OF THE MUTANT RAIN FOREST
Boston

Luiz

Born in the dense
and changing shade
of nature wilding,
perverse and surreal
in its beauty,
wherever I travel
on Earth or beyond,
the forest stains
my life and thought.
And when I sleep
safe in the shade
of civilization,
its rules and culture
and fashioned ways,
my youth returns
as a shadow dream
of emerald possession,
vital and protean
in its refrain,
darkly errant
as life unreined.

Maria

Embracing a belief
that casts the Savior
in a feline image,
she yearned to virgin

birth the Second Coming
as a bestial miracle.
Instead she has gathered
an army of urban strays,
longhaired and short,
alley to pure Siamese,
who roam her house
and cluster on her bed.
Steadfast in her fervor,
she sleeps naked beneath
a shifting coverlet
of ragged purrs and
velvet furs and claws
like thorns of faith.

Charles

He migrated from the
Chicago Dome still
green behind the ears
to discover another
variety of green
far more knowing.
He has never strayed
from the boundaries
of this wilderness
since falling prey
to its savage and
intense intoxications.
He lives in the moment
and sleeps with all
his senses alive.
You might find him

in a clearing
with knives in hand,
daubed like a native,
poised as a beast,
slaughtering some
vivid monstrosity
for its mutant meat
and mutant hide.

Kirtano

Come with me and
I will be your guide.
I will show you
tribes of albino lemurs
with iridescent eyes,
fire-breathing bats
and mushrooms that fly,
sabered panthers standing
sixteen hands high.
Do not be afraid.
These armored transports
are nearly invulnerable
Don't mind the scales
that line my flesh.
They are not contagious.
But when I command you
to look away...obey!
It is not your body
that is in danger,
but your spirit
and your mind.

GENNA TAKES A LOVER
Boston

He has become the darkest star
of her erotic obsessions,
the critical mass beyond which
her personality can no longer ascend

or even express itself.
Whenever she considers fleeing
he launches the precise sensual bullet
that slaughters her resolve and

rushes her to new heights of excitation;
he is a grave incendiary of the flesh
who ignites her neural corridors
with undivided passion.

At first ashamed of the cries
that rise so freely from her throat,
at how her limbs thrash beyond control
beneath the artful invasions of his touch,

she has since learned to embrace her abandon,
to find a sure purchase on his slippery flanks,
to revel in the fluid guttural oh-so-foreign purr
of his lavish and fiercely whispered endearments.

And now that his supernal caress has transformed
both the substance and sanctum of her nights,
she knows that no mere human lover
could ever please her again.

FLOWER GARDENING IN THE MUTANT FOREST

Frazier

You weed out pretty annuals that
the strangler columbine will devour.
You fertilize with blood and marrow.

Your prize triffid at the center
wags its tongue constantly.
Grandma starts shouting at it.

She believes its clicks and clacks
to be messages from Uncle Pieter,
lost to the verdancy surrounding you.

Tomorrow, perhaps, Big P will
uproot and stagger about the plot,
making noisy sermons to all.

But today you welcome the acidic rains.
Some flowers wither and whine
like hyenas starving in a pack,

while others sway in absolution,
glow like lambent flames ... a balm
to your obsessive green thumb.

GOING GREEN IN
THE MUTANT RAIN FOREST

Bruce Boston

Evelyn was beautiful. Evelyn was never satisfied. She'd had lovers, more than a few, probably too many. She'd had children, but none the courts would let her keep. Not that she tried very hard to keep them. With a manic and indiscriminate dedication that left little room for children, she was always embracing one dire addiction after another: a worthless man, illegal drugs, the stim-wire, some futile fantasy dream—becoming a great artist or writer or holo star—dreams beyond her means or talent. She pursued each with all of her being until she became disillusioned or bored. Then she would discard them and move on to her next obsession.

It was her old friend John who convinced her to come with him to the Mutant Rain Forest. She'd slept with him a few times, couldn't remember how many, but that was ancient history. Somehow they had remained friends over the years, perhaps because they were maladjusted to society in many of the same ways and had shared some of the same addictions.

One night John came to her one-room walkup in the Mission District. He told her about the Mutant Rain Forest, not that she didn't already know about it from the holo. John promised her adventures and riches beyond her dreams. He couldn't stop raving about the possibilities, his words spilling over one another.

Holding up one thin arm laced with old track marks, he told her he'd seen photos of diamonds and rubies as large as his fist. He either didn't know or failed to mention that such jewels were invariably mutations of the forest that dissembled their true forms to ensnare unwary travelers.

Evelyn had just abandoned kundalini yoga—it made her back hurt and gave her headaches—so she let John's wild-eyed rant seduce her. Besides, she felt ready for an adventure.

The pair took a tramp steamer south and debarked on the northern coast of what had once been Chile, where a lip of land remained the Mutant Rain Forest had yet to claim. There was a small human settlement here that catered to the needs of those who would venture into the forest. Ill-equipped with the meager provisions and weapons they could afford, Evelyn and John embarked upon their adventure.

Thanks to John, poor sad John, long since meat to some fearsome forest predator, it turned out to be the best decision of Evelyn's life.

The Mutant Rain Forest welcomed her and she was immediately at home in its presence. As soon as she entered its borders, she began to feel transformed. Evelyn swiftly adapted to the forest and rooted there for keeps.

Now her pale green leaves, tinged with lavender and aquamarine, edged with needle-sharp spines, twine upward in graceful curves about a sinewy and milky stalk.

When her scarlet flowers bloom, each reveals a miniature replica of her human face in its corolla.

Yet don't look too closely or for too long, for hers is a visage insatiable to devour mammal or reptile, bird or insect. Her leaves will enclose you and her spines inject you with a venom that will slowly digest your body, flesh, bones and all.

Evelyn is beautiful. And Evelyn is satisfied at last.

AFTER THINGS FALL APART
Frazier

A rattling cadence of bone dry leaves
Her words flow in a stuttering stream
Her voice a wind fluting under dark eaves

She stands like Noah steering the Ark
Peering into some unknowable future then
Slumps against a giant ceiba's rough bark

Her hand detaches and crawls to her feet
Releasing motes of shining black that
Drift airborne in the stifling heat

Imagine too beneath her skull of ants
A seething mass of green-gray matter
It commands by imitation and blind chance

When the rain batters her face of vapors
An insect swarm sloughs from her frame
She collapses top down like a skyscraper

Then rebuilds—a precise imago of my lost wife

CONSUMED BY THE SENTIENCE
OF THE MUTANT RAIN FOREST
Boston

I am consumed by
the sentience of the
Mutant Rain Forest,

I am transformed to
a roiling hive mind
of mutated beetles,

voracious as piranhas,
swarming like army ants,
leveling flora and fauna

in their ravenous path.
I am something of a man
and something of a beast,

a creature once-cat,
with a distended skull
and enlarged forebrain

who now walks upright,
engaged in a mortal
struggle with a panther,

trying to obliterate
the lingering image
of my animal ancestry.

I am consumed by the

sentience of the forest,
its uncommon beauty

and inescapable horror,
more than a solo sentience
but a host of warring ones

which foster an awareness
that nurtures the riotous
and unchecked rampage

of its burgeoning borders .
I am a singular copse
of acid-violet poinciana,

transient, slowly dying,
starving for sunlight
and cloaked in shadow

by the swifter growth
that surrounds me.
I am an iridescent

great horned eagle
in stratospheric flight
with the continent

spread before me,
the mottled coverlet
of viridescent plague

reaching from Amazonia,
its tentacles winding

north to Guatemala City

and south to Patagonia.
I am a thick whirlwind
of smoke that streams

from active volcanoes
in the unknown depths
of the Mutant Rain Forest,

carrying spores that
catch the jet stream,
to traverse oceans

and snow-clad summits,
to infest the Earth
with diverse mutations.

DESCENT INTO EDEN

Robert Frazier

On the morning of his thirtieth birthday, when he was haunted by dreams of an empty childhood, Marais awoke to a wind that howled offshore of the Mutant Rain Forest of Belize. It snapped his tent flap and startled him as it keened through the mangroves hemming his campsite in the interior of tiny Last Chance Cay. His stomach spasmed with dysentery. For a moment Marais was afraid that he'd soil himself and reactivate a stench like the one that had lingered over his father on his death bed.

The spasm passed. He released his breath in a loud sigh. All he wanted to do was stay healthy. All he'd ever desired was to find a place where he felt at home and accepted and well in the heart. Perhaps the moment augured good luck: a day of important discovery in his hive studies, or one unmarred by further bouts with the disease. He pulled on his jeans and crawled out into a stinging salt spray. It took him three tries to gain his feet, and once he managed, he swayed, dizzy, the edges of his thoughts sizzling and flaking away.

"Damn it," he said, and sat down by the tide line.

Damn rotten mess he was in, that's what. How did he think he could continue? Trying to shore up a fading career on a weak stomach and weak legs. Only love can wreck a human being, his father once told him, but he was turning inside out without that complication. Without anything to hold on to but his work. Always his work. He dashed water into his eye sockets and gouged them dry as if that might draw the poisons from him. Drying his face and beard on his shirt, Marais felt a bitter impatience with himself and with the world.

The sky lightened, and six rippling camp tents buoyed up from the island's shadows. Overhead, dun-colored clouds advanced in a front from the Mexican border to the north, shrouding the other cays that listed like sunken galleons behind the barrier reef. Angling through a crack, an amber ray of sunlight pierced the gloom to strike at Marais' feet. He stared at an illuminated patch of shells, the debility in his gut spreading through his body and leaving him giddy. This shaft appeared to him as such a clean sign, such a magical sign in its suddenness and accuracy, that his eyes wet, and for an instant he was living in a triumphant future wherein he'd achieved vindication, his treatises on the group mind hailed as genius, his work with the termite colonies of the Mutant Rain Forest deemed essential by his peers. He passed his palms through the beam and marveled at how it caused the golden hairs along his wrists to glow. He buried his head in these hands and imagined their radiance purifying his flesh with heat. Years of loneliness seemed to lift from his shoulders.

"You okay, mon?"

Marais jerked his head up. He squinted into the backlit face of Ilusorio Gaspar, his Carib cook. Ilusorio scratched at the insect bites under his khaki pants and along the black marble of his belly. He appraised Marais with a stare.

Marais felt embarrassed and disoriented, as if he'd been dangling on a thread of sanity for years; yet he found no contempt in Ilusorio's face, not like with the Mexican workers who called him a *blanco*. The Carib remained as emotionless as on other mornings, when he asked questions about the worksite in the jungle and the big insects. Marais leaned back on his elbows.

"I'm fine. Just a bit tired, I guess."

"I t'ink you got sick from de feefa. Eat up by all de bugs. Or maybe de rot, you see."

"The rot," Marais repeated after Ilusorio with a shudder.

He staggered to his feet and dug into his pocket for a slim bottle of orange liquid. The serum burned the back of his throat like a tongue of lava, but it was worth it, worth the fortune he'd shelled out. It fortified him against the cartilage-eating spirochete that natives called "the rot." The leishmaniasis bacterium had mutated along with the rainforest, and now only a desperate few, like himself, or the chicleros who gathered latex into ingots from the heart of the jungle, dared venture along this slip of coast linking Belize to Mexico. The disease seemed to strip its victims of humanity, and the 'rot' wounds carried the familiar smell of slow decay. Marais believed it was the most insidious fate that could befall a man.

Pierre David Marais, that's what the birth certificate said. Marais to everyone after that, because no one cared enough to call him differently. Mother hadn't. That was certain. She abandoned them when he was five, when free love soured along the Left Bank, and though he recalled her blond hair, the face felt as incomplete as the visage of a chiclero with wounds where the ears once were. Father, however, stood in vivid relief in his memory: ruddy complexion, blond gone to gray, sunken chest. He'd propped himself against the wall of their cold water flat as he cursed his wife, detailing the gruesome afflictions that should ravage her. This had jolted a younger Marais, for he couldn't imagine anything more horrible than the squalor in which they lived. Or more accursed than the hollow feeling in his gut on those nights when Father drank until he cried over his decline, and then fall from an Academy chair to the depths of a bottle of anisette. Well, he'd adopted a thick skin, hadn't he? None of those bastards would get to him again. He'd show them. He'd never considered Paris worthy of more than contempt, and he felt a closer bond to the termites of his father's studies than to his neighbors there.

After Father died of cirrhosis, Marais developed a passion for the man's theories that bordered on pathological. He held numerous entomology degrees. He gathered newer findings. Yet when his own career fell on hard times, he also found himself turning to drink. The offer of a study in the Caribbean seemed ideal: far from the radiation leaks that depopulated Europe; close to this source of mutational resurgence, and to the unnamed species of termites that ruled the jungles with a blend of aggression and colonization.

Rain sprinkled his skin. A steady patter began to stipple the surface of the ocean with overlapping circles. Marais stood and gathered driftwood with Ilusorio, and they piled it by a scorched pit scooped out of the thin soil and slag coral underneath.

"Will this weather last?" he asked as Ilusorio kneeled and blew on a pile of coals from the previous night's fire.

A flame tindered among the embers and a cloud of ashes swirled about them and over the tents. Ilusorio coughed.

"It goin' all de day, I say. And den some."

Marais clenched his fist. "Just my luck."

While Ilusorio worked against the rain, Marais woke his four diggers from the Yucatan province and questioned them through the flaps of their tents. They argued against laboring under stormy conditions, especially after two solid weeks of excavation into a hardened termite mound. Marais shook with rage, a reaction aggravated by the dysentery, and he called them out of their tents. They stood in a ragged line, dog-faced as condemned prisoners prepared to accept their fate, but when he saw how tired they were, how in need of rest, he held back any ultimatums and agreed to give them the day off. They yelled a brief cheer and shook each other's hands. They promised to work hard the next day, then staggered back into their beds.

After gathering his equipment in the boat, he told Ilusorio that he intended to motor into the study site alone. The Carib shrugged as he preserved a flame under his coffee pot by shielding the windward side of the fire with two skillets.

"No, mon. You need company."

Marais forced a laugh. "Are you tired of cleaning pans?"

"It's fine." Ilusorio kept a blank expression. "De taamites cannot cotch us on de cay like in de faarest. Nor de bad ones of de chicleros."

"But they can in there." He pointed toward the mouth of the Rio Sultriana inside a broad lagoon. "Right?"

"You see, den. It not safe to go alone."

"Okay. You're in. Saves me from having to answer all your questions at the end of the day."

Ilusorio's face lit up for a moment, and Marais wondered what it meant, if anything. The Carib wiped away the rain that caught in his black curls and ran down the dust of ashes on his forehead and over his cheeks.

"De faarest always excitin', mon."

"Yet you've avoided it these days."

"Not dis day. Not dis one."

As he drank steaming coffee and chewed a tough jerky of smoked turtle meat, Marais studied Ilusorio's face. He found no further clues to the man's mood. Certainly little toward a warming trend in their relationship.

Later, as Ilusorio pulled on a shirt and shoes for the trip, one of the Mexican workers, named Carlos, bent by the fire for some coffee.

"The others think you should know, señor. Things come up missing in our tents. Watch this Carib. And watch out for *chicleros*."

ℓ

The rain abated during the boat ride to shore and into the mouth of the Rio Sultriana. Except for a brief stop to inspect termites harvesting pollen from a gargantua palm, where a stray one bit Ilusorio on the thumb, the trip upriver passed without event. However, when Marais steered their fiberglass boat into the creeks that networked the adjacent swamp, he grew agitated, his bearings in doubt, his sense of familiarity with the surroundings lost. They traveled this way for over an hour.

A shattered gargantua saved them. Ilusorio recalled the workers' stories about the stump of jagged heartwood. Several animals had climbed over the lip rather than risk a circumvention—as Marais theorized to a silent Ilusorio—of its vast buttressing roots and whorls of body-length thorns, and the impaled carcasses froze in various testaments of decay. On one weathered skeleton, a bird with translucent flesh pecked for marrow. Marais imagined that its staccato music was a warning from the forest. Each leaf pattern, each eddy at the riverside seemed to open new possibilities for expression. He stopped his idle conversation. He grew jittery. He jumped at every sound and at each movement in his peripheral vision, for he'd ignored such omens before in the world of politics and science. They coasted in silence to a bank adjoining the fields of an abandoned cattle ranch.

Marais jumped to the muddy bank with their gear, while Ilusorio tied the boat to a fig tree. He shrugged into his protective suit, then zipped on a netted helmet. He checked the tape that sealed his gloves to his sleeves and sealed pant legs down into tight boots. After helping Ilusorio with his seals, he turned him like a mannequin and doused him with a quinine-based repellent that kept the five centimeter termites from invading their clothes.

"Looks like dis not be needed," Ilusorio stated as he sprayed Marais in turn. He pointed at the glove that covered his thumb. "De pain be not'in'. Don't effen got a welt in dere."

"But care must be taken. Especially where you step. Too many bites will cause a fever."

"Ah. Dat be de way of it, but I wanna faaget. I see dis mon once, he act crazy from de bites. T'ink de faarest speakin' to 'im."

"Yes. It's a drug the insects manufacture. Similar in structure to the ones that a voodoo priest uses to trance zombies. There are howler monkeys about the main city of mounds whose necks are ringed with such bites. When observed by binoculars, they appear docile, willing to let the termites crawl on them and latch on. Yet when our work group approaches the clearing each day, they wail and cry and pound the trees in alarm. Which unfortunately brings the termites boiling from their mounds. So far we've been confined to exploring a dead hive."

"I be lost on dat talk, mon. Keep it simple."

Marais heard what Ilusorio said, but the explanations consumed his mind. While he'd preferred the silence of minutes ago, his own voice now seemed to allay his jitters. He led them into the forest as he talked, through a low tunnel of shadow.

"I'm hoping to gather sufficient evidence to show that the termites are in fact enlisting the howlers as sentries and allies. It seems likely that the insects are sedating them."

Marais peered through Ilusorio's netting, probing for a sign that the Carib understood the repercussions this discovery would have in scientific circles throughout the world. Instead, fear and surprise twitched in the muscles of Ilusorio's face. This seemed to Marais to carry the valence of a scathing judgment. He doubted himself for a moment.

These theories, what were they in reality? A netting that obscured true observations? Maybe they kept him from the realization that he was doomed to fail, or had failed already? No doubt Ilusorio thought him mad. He hadn't commented on the detailed talk, and had kept his customary distance at all times. Spurts of acid returned to

Marais' insides, and left his legs wobbly and his chest constricted. He pushed through the feeling, forcing confident tones into his monologue.

"The most intriguing corollary to this insight is the concept of the termitary, my father's theory in fact. He was expelled from the Academy of Sciences for its genius. In the termitary, the hive is seen as one creature. Not a million individuals. Since the Carboniferous Age they've developed into a composite animal. The termites are now the blood of the hive, foraging in capillary rivers for their leafy diet. The fungus gardens within are the stomach, digesting the leaves for the bloodstream. The warriors are the defensive claws. The queen doubles as the reproductive organs. If the queen dies, so does the lineage."

Ilusorio grunted, and when they ducked through a bush, they stepped out of the darkened groves into the rain and light at the edge of another large field, the light so diffuse that it felt to Marais as if they'd passed into a world drained of color. A caucus of monkeys screeched from their tail holds in the canopy above. Their shrill notes rose above the sound of the wind and shattered Marais' concentration.

"It's the howlers," he said, motioning with his hands. "We must get to the west end of the clearing. The termites will swarm."

He followed Ilusorio as the man stepped with ease over the first of the big insects. His moves were as fluid as if he'd spent years at it. In comparison, Marais moved with drunken rhythms. He remembered how long it had taken him to get the hang of it, and he reconsidered Ilusorio's comments from earlier that morning.

This man knew the jungle. No doubt about. He'd spent two weeks trying to master this trick, and Ilusorio could walk it in his sleep. Why had everything come hard to him? Always hard. It didn't seem fair.

The wind intensified, nosing deep into the tree canopy and rattling limbs heavy with leaves. Rain pelted the clearing. The ground was mired where the termites had stripped away its grassy cover.

"Damn! I didn't think it would rain like this."

"We not lookin' to de sky. De signs be dere."

The rain fell in veils of silver that swirled about Marais and obscured his view. A solid sheet lashed at him. It threatened to topple him to the ground.

"We've got to find cover!" Marais yelled.

The two men pushed back the way they'd come, with Marais crushing a few stragglers in the termite's own retreat. Instead of re-entering the tunnel through the forest, Ilusorio waved him toward another opening where the thickets had blown down to reveal a rotted fence row and a crumbling building in the distance. In the inky shadows of the thickets, Marais spotted termites by their glow. When Ilusorio stopped to stare at one, he had to tug the Carib along the fence, explaining the bioluminous phenomenon with garbled shouts into the gale. They fought the weather until they were exhausted.

The hacienda that once ruled over the ranch lands had fallen into abject ruin, and its shape suggested the stump of a gargantua. The clearing that once surrounded it had given way to crimson-barked fig trees under-storied by graceful horsetails, while liana vines reclaimed the structure, threading into the broken windows like power lines punched through by the jungle. It looked to Marais as if they fed the structure a green light, yet when they pushed aside the broken door, and huddled in the entry, he realized the source was outside—muted sunlight passing through an overgrown hole in the roof. He slumped against a wall, setting his pack on a roll of peeled wallpaper for a backrest.

"We lucky 'bout dis place. No sign of snakes."

Marais nodded. "Especially lucky if the storm keeps up. It might cover us while we observe the lived-in hives."

"Dat's so. But den we may haff to stay de nite."

As if to emphasize Ilusorio's statement, the wind blew the door shut against the jam with a solid crack. Marais sat upright.

"Relax, mon. De aftaanoon grow long."

Marais appreciated his concern, and he felt a momentary bond of brotherhood with this stranger. It felt good. The Mexican's warning about Ilusorio, though well-intended, seemed also to be ill-founded. The Carib passed into the next room, leaving him to rest.

The rain continued to pelt the forest, drumming the roof above and an exposed floor somewhere in the guts of the building. The rhythms lulled Marais. He nodded off, dreamed of his life as a boy. In this life, though, he and his father lived in a huge red tree house, high in the tallest maple of a park along the Seine. Scholars and scientists gathered below to listen to his father's speeches. They were invited up while Marais served wine or tea. They patted him on the shoulder and brought their daughters for him to meet. They were his family, and the whole world his address. And they never forgot a birthday.

❦

Marais swam up through sodden levels of drowsiness. He followed the sound of a moan. Raising his head from his knees, he shook out the cobwebs of sleep, and then ate dried fruit and crackers from his pack. The sound became a murmuring voice; this time it wasn't a dream. He thought he heard his name whistle through the eves as the storm continued outside and the sun dimmed to a faint presence, thickening into violet washes that alarmed him. He couldn't stand the thought of being trapped. He knew that they should run for the boat and recover emergency supplies, if not make an attempt at returning to the tents on Last Chance. He needed his serum and his men.

"Ilusorio! Ilusorio where are you?"

The murmur grew louder.

"Ilusorio. Is that you?"

Marais pushed himself to his feet though sharp pains lanced his ankles. He tore down his socks where the rain had washed away the repellent and loosened the taped seals, and he used his gloves to crush a crowd of fat termites that bit into the soft flesh about his heels.

"Jesus!"

His head pinwheeled.

"Ilusorio?"

Marais stepped from the hall into a bare room that amplified the mysterious voice. At the far end of the room he found a metal stairway that spiraled up through a column of pale light, where the roof had collapsed and the rain flashed in drips from the growths that choked the roof hole, slicking the mossy stairs. He held the handrail as he climbed. His ascent seemed to corkscrew into the column, carrying him to a heaven of weak illuminations and unkempt gardens, and only after several turns in the stairs did he realize that the illusion was enhanced by a large snake—a golden boa mutated to the thickness of a tree trunk—that slid down the central shaft as he went up. Marais felt dizzy, and he hurried to the landing above.

He rubbed the spots from his eyes, and he stepped into a large unfinished space. On a desk stood the shell of an antique computer, one of the early Macintosh models whose intact screen glowed with shifting light. As Marais approached it, fascinated by the impossibility of light without electric power, the voice that had awakened him rattled from the computer box and startled him. He noted the signs of termites where they'd tunneled into the disk drive slot. The light and sound appeared to be the revelations of the insects that moved within the machine, the essences of their tiny lives channeled through the senses of the circuitry, and as he swiveled the chair, intending to sit before the computer, he came face to face with a swarthy man. Or at least the semblance of one. The chiclero's nose and ears were rotted away, and his head slumped against the backrest. Whether recently dead or in a deep coma, he was gone from the world, his skin drained of color, yet he twitched on occasion. A feat, Marais realized, that could only be accounted for by the termites lodged at the nerve centers on his neck and under his tattered clothes. The head jerked sideways and the eyes fluttered open. They fixed on the screen as if decoding a message from the shifting patterns within. Marais followed its hollow stare and found that the bioluminous termites formed a face in the screen, the face of his father. It tried to speak to him.

Marais backed away, terrified yet fascinated. The corpse's head jerked again, and its eyes were glowing, ringed with larval termites. Marais bolted. He tore through the growth on the stairs and slipped his way down to the first floor until he ran headlong into the wall at the bottom. His helmet cushioned some of the blow. His skull the rest.

⁋

When Marais awoke this time it was pitch black in the hacienda, and many hours had passed. His temples throbbed, but the ache was dull and distant, healed by many hours of dreamless oblivion. He pulled on his helmet, shoved through the main door into the overgrown yard. Marais could see his way toward the termites' clearing in the faint airglow outside. By now the bites he'd incurred and the blow to his head had left him feverish, unsure of his own thoughts or the things that he saw, yet he considered the boat a reasonable escape and a necessary one. Then he heard Ilusorio's voice calling from ahead. He jogged down the old driveway.

"Marais. Help me."

Marais jogged faster, hands before him, pushing through a torrent of leaves stirred up from the ground by a strong gust. His helmet tumbled off his head and rolled away on its edge. The voice called again, and he followed it down a side trail that led away from the house and the excavations. The voice said to hurry. He ran harder, blocking out the pain that shot up through his calves. Marais pushed through unfamiliar territory until he entered a rent in the forest, a shadowy counterpart to the one populated with hive mounds. In this one, a single gargantua pointed a crooked finger into the faint washes of dawn, and a massive hive mound wound around it, using its girth to support the largest colony he'd ever seen. Ilusorio stood at the base of this tower—without protective clothing—and coughed as he held his belly.

"Are you alright?" Marais asked as he approached, out of breath.

"Yes. Oh, yes." Ilusorio's voice sounded like he was drifting on narcotics. "And now de old one wanna see you. He been waitin'."

"Waiting? What's going on?"

"Dis an impaatant nite. You impaatant. You must climb de birt'in' mound and meet your fate."

Two stocky chicleros—Mestizos in better shape than the one in the ranch house—stepped from the shadows and tied Marais' arms behind him. They removed his gloves. He struggled, but his muscles lacked strength.

Ilusorio said, "I'm sorry," and motioned him to follow, and Marais was pushed onto a narrow ledge that wound up the hardened wall of the mound and about the trunk of the gargantua. A fresh squall dashed him with cold slugs of rain. He shivered and stared at Ilusorio's back as the wind seemed to urge him up the crude steps.

A bolt of lightning crackled across the sky. This illuminated the Carib and highlighted a bulge that ringed his belly under his shirt. In the darkness that followed, Marais noticed a faint glow there, and when the wind ruffled the edge of Ilusorio's shirt tail, it revealed the foxfire-white bodies of termites hanging from his belly skin. Remembering the bites he'd seen there that morning, Marais swore, but his anger over Ilusorio's betrayal soon waned. It wore away with the tedious climb. This turn of events only cemented his belief that the jungle had held the key to his fate all along.

As they mounted a flattened lip at the top of the mound, which looked out over the jungle treetops and into the top of the gargantuan, which had been completely eaten away, Marais stumbled forward. Ilusorio shoved him into the hole, following close behind. A bolt of lightning arced in blue across the sky, forking like a skeletal hand. They stood on wet sawdust and hardened cellulose to face a hooded figure twenty yards away on the opposite side of the lip. The figure spoke to them over the thunder.

"You've brought him, Ilusorio."

"Just as you say. Just as de sick one upstairs at de ranch say."

"You will be rewarded. Go. Take the others to our retreat in the interior. The blanco and I will follow."

Ilusorio gave Marais a quick glance, hung his head, and melted into the darkness. The figure turned to Marais.

"So, you know of us, señor. You've studied us."

Marais tried to cover his ears, but the voice penetrated his barrier and bore its way inside his thoughts.

"Come closer."

The pain in his ankles flared, spread through his body. He felt himself respond to the command. The old one held a power over him. He seemed to float with the feeling, and found himself against the far lip of the bowl with his head even with the knees of the old one.

"Are you ready to join us? To join us wholly?"

Marais knew then that the termitary wanted him as a part, as an extension of itself. He was a man who understood it better than anyone from the outside world could. He understood hive imperatives, and could act as an ambassador for it. Or an agent. The pain eased within him at this thought, even the grumbling threads of dysentery quieted in his gut. All his life he'd wanted siblings and a real home. This was the first offer he'd ever had. The first gesture of acceptance. He felt a tug of longing in his heart.

"You want an initiate," he said.

"You're already initiated, Señor Marais. You've felt our sting." The voice grated on him the way his father's had during the last days, when he'd lapsed into rabid curses that called for Marais' mother.

"Do you join? Answer." The voice wailed with the wind, seeming to unravel into exotic names for disease and death. "Step forth."

Marais knew what it meant to join. He'd been the only one to embrace his father's theories on the potentials of the hive mind, and now he was asked to put his faith to the test. He'd been asked into the family.

"Yes," he responded, and with that he felt the termites swarming up about his feet. "No!"

He looked up with tears in his eyes, hoping for a sign from the sky like the clean ray of light he'd found that morning. Thunder rumbled in the direction of the river. More brilliant flashes of lightning. A gust blew back the hood of the old one above him. It was not his father, if indeed it was now a man at all. Leishmaniasis had taken not only his nose and ears, but in some way stripped the flesh from his skull, then eaten back the softened bone and exposed the brain.

Marais froze in awe. The figure before him appeared to be an interface between man and the termitary, an ancient human whose life was extended by his link to the hive. His features were grooved where the feet of termites made their daily route. The eyes looked pupil-less and milky white, with lids stitched by hanging fragments of moss. Rotted wounds were tended by termites that grew fungal salads at their edges, and his brain was transformed into a fungus-draped organ that squirmed under their ministrations like a queen laying eggs. The old Mestizo embodied the evolutionary step from a human form to a greater form of being. This went beyond the possibilities of group mind that Marais had fought in vain to prove to the world, beyond what he thought plausible.

"Decide, blanco. You can not be allowed to leave with your knowledge of us."

The ancient one bent toward him. Overcome with the heat of revelation, Marais reached up to the old one and gripped his arms as he bent further. The man lost his balance, tumbled and bounced off his head into the glowing termites and larvae boiling about him. Marais felt his skull explode. His mind seemed charged with sudden clarity and pain. With his senses clear, Marais breathed the horrid odor of the man's flesh; it smelled like death and fecal decay. It smelled like his distant past. Again the old one reached for Marais, but he kicked the man back in revulsion, and hoisted himself onto the lip of the mound. He beat the insects off him as more poured from the opening over the old one. The roof of the mound collapsed away from the lip under the combined weight, and he saw the man's arms flail up for a moment, offering, perhaps, a physical manifestation of his disbelief at Marais' decision. As the old one disappeared, there was a loud cry from the clearing below. Several chicleros shouted as they scrambled up toward him along the ledge that spiraled about the hive.

In the eye of the storm, whose calm equaled the ravages of a normal storm, Marais slipped down the side of the mound in big jumps, surprising the chicleros and reaching the jungle trails at the perimeter of the clearing before them. From there on it was a wild race. He listened to the voice of the wind as it led him. He prayed that the drenching fury that bent the trees to submission would also provide cover for his escape. After each flash of lightning more distant than the last, he saw that he negotiated less of unfamiliar territory and entered upon more of the old ranch lands where his studies had centered. He also saw the faces of his pursuers growing near, with a tall, swift man in the lead. This first man caught him for a moment, grabbing around his chest, trying to pull him down. Marais was so slippery with rain that he managed to twist out of the man's grip and shoulder him aside. The man up-ended, impaled on a long gargantua thorn.

With a surge of adrenalin and several bold strokes of fortune, Marais emerged alone on the riverbank where the boat was tied, collapsing into the extra gear stored at the stern. The rainwater that collected there slopped against him. He felt renewed by the squalls that stung his face, and he lay for the briefest moment on his back as the drug-induced grip of the termitary ebbed from his body. But shouts reverberated through the forest shadows, causing him to jerk upright. Gunshots followed. Frantically, he strapped his big flashlight to the bow and started the boat on its way.

Another motor started up behind him. A bullet pinged off his hull.

With the same luck, heightened less now by the madness of the night and more by his fear that the engine might stall, Marais pushed the boat along the choppy river at full throttle. The beam of his flashlight rose and fell through the overhanging growths like a machete slashing its way to freedom. The dugout behind him kept pace but could not close the gap, and the few shots that were fired missed their mark in the rough conditions. He reached the mouth of the river as the sun leaked above the forest, a bloodshot eye peeking between the canopy top and the dispersing storm front. It seemed to rise from a shattered underworld below the horizon. The rain stopped at last.

The dugout fell behind in the bigger chop of the sea. Marais pushed his engine to its limits. His men heard the boat as he motored close into the shallows near their campsite on the tiny island, and they poured from the tents to meet him. He screamed to them about the evil chicle gatherers and pointed at the approaching dugout. They fired a pistol at the chicleros, but had to duck for cover when one of them caught a rifle bullet in the leg in the return volley. Marais dug into his boat gear and pulled out a flare gun. Taking careful aim as his three pursuers plowed toward his mooring, he nailed the flare charge into the center of the dugout. It erupted in flame and exploded when the extra gas tanks caught fire. None of the three surfaced alive.

"Ah, Señor," Carlos said as he slapped Marais on the back. "You are a brave man. To fight them like that. And to have slept in the jungle at night."

The other Mexicans let out a loud cheer. They carried him to the main tent and poured coffee and rum between his chattering lips. They jostled him, wrapped him in colorful Indian blankets. They cajoled him into telling his story, looking awestruck at his revelations of the forest and at the account of his escape from the chicleros and the old one. Carlos nodded in agreement as Marais told them how bitter he felt about Ilusorio. He'd become someone different in the eyes of these men: a hero and a friend. He found in their excited faces a validation that had been missing from his life. In one day—an exact twenty four hours—he'd rejected a chance to prove his work, to live at the very core of the theory of communality that had driven his father and nearly himself to ruin in the civilized world. Now, he'd found a deeper, seemingly more resolute companionship with these men than he'd considered possible. For with all their faults, and no doubt because of them, they were human. They were familiar in all ways that warmed him deeply, warmed some catacomb in his heart that he'd long given up as remote, cold, and lost to anything less than a miracle.

"It was as I feared," Carlos said when the others broke open another bottle of rum. He sighed, his eyes locked on Marais in a thoughtful, knowing look. "The Carib betrayed you."

"But you have not," he told Carlos.

If in the future he should consider himself at home in the world, triumphant or not, Marais knew that the feeling began there on Last Chance Cay. He relaxed at last, content to repeat his adventures to them over and over.

THE MUTANT RAIN FOREST MEETS THE SEA
Boston

All-night cantinas are still.
Shabby *film-noir* hotels
are steeped in shadow
deeper than their stains.

The vines are everywhere,
like the scouts of an army
hard upon their heels,
like mad organic lace,

a grand ophidian opulence
leafing the listing
masts that dot the harbor,
caging the empty plazas

and abandoned streets
in tendrils that strayed
along pastel walls,
across rust tile roofs,

twining through windows
with sinuous grace,
toppling lamps aside,
indifferent to remains,

mute green strength,
blind and vegetative,
about to pull the city
down into its waves.

A COMPASS FOR THE MUTANT RAIN FOREST

Boston/Frazier

Norte

Along the dense extremities of the forest north
that advance across the Panamanian Isthmus,
ancient bridge for mustang, panther, and bear,
the trunks of towering andirobas intertwine
interminably in unfettered mahogany abandon.

Their barks are host to a protean foxfire that
radiates iconographic images in a flowing
expressionist relief of mythic proportions.
Travelers who venture this trek witness
these mutations and are soon transfixed.

Denied hopes coalesce, enrapture the weary.
Anguished women cradle the luminous souls
of dead babies and old friends half forgotten
in this swirling meccano of empires and loves.
the wasted alternatives of life are unveiled.

Though indios and neobiologists urge them
to flee the hypnotic force of such coercions,
these errant pilgrims prostrate themselves in
a mad chorus of wails and call the forest wall
Mural del Dios Verde, Mural of the Green God.

Sur

Along the avaricious trail of the forest south,
to the steep windswept cliffs of Patagonia

that rise ragged above rock-strewn beaches,
the emerald hunger stretches farther still
to taint the freezing waters off Cape Horn.

The winds that rake these seas now blow
from the north, warm, fragrant with pollen,
as if the forest could root on the icy cap.
Glassine flounder and neon frogs rain down
to pummel the decks of passing steamers.

But the gun-crack calving of melting bergs
and the slow thaw that extends the sea's reach
expose no sure foothold for the forest to claim.
Even the shapeshifting *woohli* has yet to adapt
to the rough hibernal currents of this ocean.

The polar mariners who sail this route watch
the skies, cross themselves, shake their heads,
wonder if the next storm will be even stranger.
Beneath their breaths they curse the forest as
El Diluvio del Diablo, The Deluge of the Devil.

Este

Along the clawing tendrils of the forest east
that cloak the Amazon and its serpentine
tributaries—Madeira, Jacunda, Japurá—
once thriving passages for trade and travel,
only the most bestial of tribes now survive.

At dusk from the hills of Macapá and Belém
you can see the flicker of their campfires
against the gravid green of a dark horizon.

In less than a generation they have morphed
with the forest and are no longer human.

Forging a symbiosis with the force that
rules their world, some are viridescent,
mimicking the foliage that surrounds them.
Others, covered with bony plates, often
prey on all fours like porcine armadillos.

From Caracas in the North to the ramshackle
slums of Rio and Sao Paulo and Buenos Aires,
those who remain in the coastal enclaves call
the forest *Creación Oscura*, Dark Creation,
El Enfermo, Diseased One, *Salvaje*, Savage.

Oeste

Along the sweltering frontiers of the forest west,
striping the Andean foothills with wide shadows
and blanketing their no longer snowy heights,
the spikes of thousand-meter bromeliads sway
like the minarets of an organic metropolis.

The great reaches of flora that line these
slopes seem to roar in their rushing before
opening the cores of their inflorescence and
clasping entire settlements in a snap embrace.
A tenderizing mucilage bathes their spoils.

Those who flee this furious onslaught take
refuge in the lightless swamplands below and
return to pay homage, seeing these carnivorous
plants as rampant evolution running in reverse,

mankind succoring and serving the landscape.

The pathetic pageantry of their stark display
culminates in a sacramental sharing of pulcre,
an hallucinogen brewed from this succulent.
Stray revelers whisper the forest's name as
La Bestia Caprichosa, The Capricious Beast.

Profundidades

In the impermeable fortress of the forest depths,
where each generation of growth destroys the last,
where each generation of fauna devours the last,
a sentience amoral and earthly dreams that the
only word for forest is *el Mundo*, the World.

THE MUSIC OF THE MUTANT RAIN FOREST
Boston

is a completely natural music
born of transformation,

a thoroughly mutated music
born from corruption.

The Mutant Rain Forest
comes alive at night,
and that is when
its orchestra tunes up
in a wild cacophony
of unnatural selection:

the hissing baritone
of a millipede python

the hypnotic drone
of the blood orchid,
drawing predators
that become prey,

the rising falling hum
of insect swarms
as they live and die
and evolve into
twilight dawn,

the raucous squeak
of the parrot hawk,
a ravenous bird,
a shadow bird

except when it feeds
and a feathered ruff
rises in garish
rainbow array
around its neck,

the hard bone click
of horned tapirs
clashing by night
for control of the herd,
the roars that
rake their throats,

and always
the sudden intermittent
sounds of death and feeding,
the cries of the conquest
and of those eaten.

And intertwined and echoing
within and beyond it all,
the sibilant and husky
language of the cat people,
a constant refrain,
whispering yet insistent
in its seductive complexity.

For no rational reason
you wait for them to finish,
but they go on and on,
this endlessly tuning up

You wait for the
conductor to appear

in his tie and tails
with baton in hand,
tapping the stand
for attention
and silence.

You wait for him
to raise his arms
and strike that
hard blow
against the air
with his stick
that starts the concert.

But he never does.

There is
no conductor.
The concert
never begins.

And that arrhythmic
beat keeps changing
with every measure.

You are frightened
yet drawn by
its random oscillations
and savage insinuations.

Then you realize
that you are already
listening to the concert,
this endless tuning up

for a performance
that never occurs
and occurs forever.

IT'S OKAY TO LISTEN TO THE GREEN VOICE
Frazier

& I ask you how many dreams remain when the forest's
     music is held remote
withheld beyond the thought-barrier of the ventricles

how many lost before the demon amphibian god
     of stone rhythm
van de graaf's its white rhisomous capillary antennae

these beams of scalar order can disarm our nerve tree
massage the deep red tissues of our composure

the infection moves through the fine motors of the wrist
the whorls of a hundred identities hum at our fingertips

st. vitus light leaks from each skin silo
each pavement scar in the blood trailways

down in the mansions of dna the staircases unravel
in the cell camps the soul unstrangles

hammered strings fibrillate mingus pastorius monk
baselines of articulation black and molecular

yeah the milford graves of beat lashes out
brass stops spew ghost notes dolphy notes

and unleashed in a firestorm of heat imaging
chernobyled from the hidden place with no center

we are all blurs of hysteria across the stage
avatars of the least emotion

the music bumps swell on our foreheads
ready to exceed limit

and all this all this mind you
happens in a moment of recognition

when just the right phrase of adrenalin
washes over from the unexpected

from the arpeggio white noise of metal
from the silver throat of a macaw

from the claymore of some mutated throat
from across the tripwires of tomorrow

from the genes of change
you never thought you contained

AERIAL RECONNAISSANCE
OF A CONFLAGRATION AT THE
HEART OF THE MUTANT RAIN FOREST

Bruce Boston & Robert Frazier

Rainbow flocks whorl in a maelstrom of feathers over the drifting gray incontinence of smoke. Primaried macaws. The blinking of neon toucans. A transparent ibis with lungs visibly pumping. The milky glistening flight of albescent eagles. Dipping its prop into avian shadows upon the haze like a beast testing the ebon acid of the Styx, our craft volplanes across the immense fire site. Ascending hordes of bats and winged toads alight upon the plane's fuselage, causing the old woman who accompanies us to start back from her view. Their suckered paws are slime pink upon the glass, the scrabbling of their razor claws like hail.

> *Deep in the heartland of this prodigal wilderness,*
> *carved from massive trunks and structured from*
> *the shaping and rechanneling of living growth,*
> *a biotic metropolis waits on the blackened horizon.*

Tapering clouds of doomed insects flume past us, darkling twisters that surge with disparate energy and often explode in tempests of chitinous flak. More subtle are the flickering tendrils of flame that flare up and die, flare up and die, beckoning like the arms of demons urging us to join them below. Our compass is set on the heart of the conflagration. The plane banks, and the old woman begins to speak of the tribe she claims to have discovered there. She cries for a lover who stayed behind to study and learn, to help build a mecca in green hell. Her rumored madness surfaces in hoarse whispers of another lover "who tamed my soul, who plundered my senses, whose acrid feline touch left my womb fused and barren as the sand of a nuclear range."

> *Deep in the prodigal heartland of the mutant forest,*
> *their city offers a symbiosis of fauna and flora,*
> *an architectonic pastiche of budding vegetation*
> *that changes even as we record its singularity.*

As we navigate the high walls of particulate gloom, our passage delivers us into a clearer air space, dotted by wispy plumes and whirlwinds of ash. The terrain beneath is etched in startling contrasts. An altered plain stretches ahead toward further haze. The evidence of past burnings outlines rugged byways. Rectangular viridian patches have survived everywhere, now peppered with a thickening coat of cinder falls and edged in solarized yellow from the extreme heat. As the stench of organic incineration fills the cabin, fumbling in her flight jacket the old woman extracts the crudely wrought crucifix of an impaled panther, a religious symbol outlawed in the Northern Cities. Her parchment hands caress the graven image tenderly.

We note how the fire has traveled Hydra-like up trunk valleys and along the course of rivers, scaling mountains for a foothold in farther realms, as if colonizing the landscape with its fiery brand yet sparing the main clumps of forest for another fate. Our pilot calls it unnatural and crosses himself twice. The old woman follows suit, clutching the hideous icon to her withered breasts, and begins to chant an incantation in a voice no longer recognizable as human, a crescendo of gutturals, hisses, and glottal stops which culminates in a soprano animal screech that sets my teeth on edge. At last we admit that we are in the presence of one, regardless of her sanity, who understands far more of the world below than we may ever be able to fathom.

As we emerge from a churning bank of dark cumuli, seeded by smoke and thickening across the center, we spot an immense tree—no, a score of trees, twining together like vines reaching for the light. Gathered about the circumference of this Ydrigsal, slashing with unbounded energy at its woody tissues, work parties of cats stand, tall and deceptively lean, taming the errant growth into dwellings and streets. Their fur is matte black with a sleek bluish sheen. And beyond their endeavor the burgeoning city waits beneath a sky where smoke and burning ash do not sail, where we can watch the dwindling white circumference of our passenger's parachute as it drifts earthward past slender ceiba towers and liana-draped terraces, florescent with the bloom of unknown mutant strains.

*Deep within our hearts the prodigal past haunts
our imagination, we rue our tainted histories
and the destructions we must claim
as the fire-dampening storm begins to wail.*

CONFIRMED BY THE MUTANT RAIN FOREST
Boston

You travel to the Mutant Rain Forest
fleeing the artificial environments
that have formed and framed your life,
seeking fortunes worldly and spiritual,

hoping to rediscover pristine nature
or perhaps merely another sensation
to further tease your jaded palate.
You travel to the Mutant Rain Forest

spurred by hungers you cannot sate,
seeking flavors you have yet to savor.
Here you encounter a terra incognita
where the skills you have mastered

are irrelevant, where ideologies fog
and scatter, where the protracted
evolutionary climb from sea to land,
from fish to beast to civilized man,

provides no shelter, no saving grace.
Here your humanity triggers your fate.
In the heart of the Mutant Rain Forest
where marvelous circumstance abounds,

you must stand naked and begin again.
In the wilds of the Mutant Rain Forest
where protean life stalks and feasts,
your stray passage is such likely prey.

In the dark of the Mutant Rain Forest
phantasmagoric visions fall like rain:
vile apparitions, angelic intimations,
discrepant as the epitaphs you crave.

BROMELIAD BRAIN
Frazier

A 3-pound hub for synaptic grubs
How much fires in the end
We can't know the extent

But with lime spiders et al and
Their blinding webs as linkage
Maybe it can attain sentience

Naked to the weather
High in the forest canopy
It feeds on everything

Reaching for the sun's degrees
Or for the incinerating fields
Of love's human corona

DESERTED ALTARS
IN THE MUTANT RAIN FOREST
Boston

In the deep shadows
of the Mutant Rain Forest,
rough stone altars
shrouded by indigo moss
still bear the stains
of blood ritual.

Mortal sacrifice
did not sate
the gods once
worshipped here,
but the reverence
it reflected did.

Now they wait
in the Mutant Rain Forest,
shadows of their
former selves,
frail as waifs
in their abandonment.

Now they dream
through drowsy decades,
in a hypnagogic state,
dreams red and rich
with ritual slaughter.

Abandoned in the
Mutant Rain Forest,
imprisoned in stone,

draped with indigo moss,
they wait for true believers,
some new transient species,
to evolve out of the wilderness
and worship at their altars
with blood sacrifice
once more.

DAS SENSIBLE CHAOS
Frazier

adapting from natural to global
invading conduits, phone boxes, homes
these mites from the rainy canopies

in fiber optics fine and bright as angel hair
they will generate a shroud for the living

mottled with the colorful husks of their dead
it exudes plasms both luminous & psychoactive

one touch will stagger you
under the color wheel of heaven

Mandelbrot patterns shift in the violence
a Rorschach with infinite possibility

stare too long at the texture & your thoughts
seem suspect in their affect on the weave

illustrations of your failures & futures
emerge with nightmarish detail

yet to rend the work proves fruitless
their networked efforts redouble

while a mask for your last hours gathers
from the broken lightless spokes

SURROUNDED BY
THE MUTANT RAIN FOREST

Bruce Boston

A weak December sun falls like a faltering beacon against the shadows that surround us. We enter another vine-choked alley. The red breath of our laser rifles sizzles through the intrusion of leaves, blackening them to ash. The forest is driven back one more time, but we know it will return.

Once we lived as civilized residents of a civilized metropolis. Now we retreat, losing ground to the mutations of the wild. As their multifarious forms proliferate, their mythology invades our lives, a compulsion for those who embrace the heresy of a bestial faith, a prison for those of us who resist the onslaught. We survive as a pocket of humanity in a deluge of green terror, cut off from the North, facing a relentless enemy from the South. Already more than a third of the city has been abandoned to the wilds.

扳

On a routine sweep of City Center I find her in a decaying subbasement of the old Opera House where the classic tragedies of Verdi and Donizetti had once been performed. The beam of my torch momentarily blinds her dark eyes, unaccustomed to the light. I can see from her stricken glance that she is one the Mutant Rain Forest has made good use of. She has become a tragedy all her own. The stalk binding her bare body to the bare dirt, a curve both graceful and horrific as it clings to the base of her spine, resembles that of a mushroom, thick and spongy, white blotched by patches of gray. And she is now its naked human cap.

My happenstance comrades, roaming the deserted stage and hallways above, sound the all-clear. And after a moment of indecision I answer in kind, turning my torch away from her eyes, leaving her to the shadows of her damp fungal hermitage and whatever monstrosity she has become. Not a word is exchanged between us.

Of course I recognize her in those flash seconds, despite the intervening years and how pale she has become. Yet it is only hours later in the dim hall of the barracks, lying sleepless on my cot among the unending noise of sleeping men—snores and sighs and dream whimpers—that I replay the details of our past together.

A wealthy landowner's daughter and the son of a servant, we played together as children. The forest was distant then, no more than a threat sometimes used to frighten us into obedience. We played together for hours and days on end, oblivious to our origins. Until time and age made them manifest, forcing the adult world into our existence. Then she left me behind for a life of private tutors and trips abroad, a privileged world I was never allowed to enter.

Still I watched from afar as the girl I had known began to mature into a woman. And fool that I was, I nurtured an adolescent infatuation that I called love. I embarked upon an awkward courtship, sending her furtive notes to which she never responded. I once stood beneath her lighted window with a cheap guitar and serenaded her with a cheap love song. Only the night answered. And eventually her father's rage, who insisted that such nonsense must come to an end.

My thoughts had returned to her more than once over the years. Wistful and unfulfilled. Now I wonder what hazardous course her life had taken that has transformed her to a prisoner and slave of the forest. I know that her father is no longer the wealthy landowner, that the forest has long since claimed his cultivated fields and mansion. Yet how has it seduced her when I had failed? Harboring vague regrets, I drift into a restless sleep.

℞

I wake to a scream engendered by someone's nightmare. I don't realize I am the culprit, the scream my own, until I hear the exclamations and curses of those around me that I have also awakened. Whatever that dark dream, it instantly flees from my consciousness. Yet my troubled sleep has formed a resolution in my mind.

I dress hurriedly in the dimness and make my way to our makeshift armory. There I choose a machete whetted razor sharp. When I test its edge a small drop of blood purls upon my finger. With my laser rifle strapped across my shoulder and the machete shoved into my belt, I enter the dark streets.

It is a cold night and a bone-raking chill fills the air, heightened by a light yet steady wind from the south that carries the fragrances of the Mutant Rain Forest into the city. Some claim that it is only this cold that protects us from the forest's ruthless onslaught. They say that with the rains of spring and the heat of summer the mutations of the forest, both animal and vegetable, will thrive. They will grow more profligate and insistent, attacking with renewed vigor.

Others of my kind, those who sleep by day and guard the city by night, now patrol the streets.

I pass freely among them, nodding or exchanging greetings with those I know. I make my way to City Center and the old Opera House, a hulking shadow against a cloud-clotted sky that absorbs and diffuses the city lights. There are no stars visible.

As I descend into the depths of the building, my torch guiding me, I begin to shiver. It seems even colder here than in the streets above. I have decided that I will either free her from her enslavement or end her life trying, for surely death is a fate preferable to the one she now endures.

I find her as I had before, in the same dank subterranean chamber. This time, as my torch exposes her naked body, she gives out a short sharp cry, more avian than human. Yet her eyes do not blink from the light. Instead, they meet mine in a grave and curious stare. I wonder if she knows who I am, if she recognizes me from our shared past. In my fatigues, with my untrimmed beard and shaggy hair, I appear a far different man than the youth she once knew. Just as she must be a far different woman, if woman you could still call her. I wonder how much of her mind and thoughts remain or if her human awareness has been completely stripped away by the forest.

I approach her and raise the machete. Yet as my arm descends to sever the stalk that binds her body to the dirt, she reaches out swiftly to grasp and hold my wrist with a strength I did not expect from her slender form. The blade falls from my hand.

She rises up, her arms encircling my neck, and pulls me down toward her. She begins soundlessly showering my face and neck with kisses. And fool that I once was, fool that I remain, I fall to my knees beside her, dropping the torch and returning her embrace. It rolls away, throwing its beam against a rough stone wall, leaving us in relative darkness. Her bare flesh is not cold but warm to the touch, radiating a heat all its own, stripping the chill from my body. Her mouth and tongue are feverish and urgent.

Lying by her side, I awkwardly remove my clothes with one hand, holding her close to me with the other. Although I do not know if she is human or an extension of the forest, it no longer matters. My reason is lost, my senses trapped by a rising passion that has endured for years without consummation. I begin whispering endearments to her in the dark, speaking her name over and again. She does not answer. No sound escapes her lips except for her heavy breathing and the sighs of passion. Then I enter her and although my body and senses remain engaged in an act both terrifying and sublime, my mind and my vision are all at once traveling elsewhere.

I take on the form of a great bird of keen eye and iridescent plumage sailing high above the Earth, flying through the stratosphere, far higher than any bird has a right to fly. I see the continent spread beneath me, the mottled blanket of mutant infestation stretching forth from the Amazon Basin to cover near half the land, its tentacles snaking north to the Isthmus and south to Patagonia. I swoop lower and am suddenly plummeting downward through dense green leaves and a riotous florescence of blossoms to the forest floor. I am a horned jaguar standing over sixteen hands high, gliding sinuously through the foliage, my nostrils flared, testing the fragrances of the thick night air in search of prey. I am a millipede python, dropping hundreds of feet through the tortuous branches of a towering mahogany onto the muscular back of that same jaguar, my spurred legs digging through its fur and into its flesh, injecting a soporific venom, my body winding round its torso, crushing the breath from its body. I am a miniature winged albino monkey, no, a whole tribe of winged albino monkeys, a hive mind, flitting and leaping and chattering through the highest branches of that same tree. I am a copse of huge black and gold orchids being devoured to extinction by a herd of ravaging tapirs, their variegated hides shaded by saffron and amber and celadon. It is as if through the union of our bodies the forest and its manifold incarnations are speaking to me, immersing me in their beauty and their horror. I am imbued with the sentience of the forest, not a singular sentience as some believe, but a thousand warring ones that conspire to a whole, eliciting an overriding consciousness that wars against the world at large, as if the acts of slaughter and consumption within its borders, the endless round of creation and death and recreation, provide it with further sustenance and growth. And as my final thrusts within her seal our union, I am hurled from the sum of that consciousness into exhaustion and down the black well of a dead sleep.

ᘔ

And it is blackness to which I awaken. I have no idea how many minutes or hours have passed. The batteries in the torch have run down while I slept and we lie together in complete darkness. I try to rise only to find her body rising with me, pulling me back to the earth. I feel a sharp pain along my chest and stomach and thighs. I cry out and she cries with me, in that same piercing avian tone I heard before. Reaching between us I feel the ropey fungal tendrils that have spread from her flesh to mine. In rising panic, I grapple for the machete, but wherever it has fallen, it is beyond my reach. And it is probably useless in any case. Even if I could stand the pain of severing those tendrils, I am no doubt already infected as she.

So I wait in the dark, bound irretrievably to a lover I have desired and sought for so long. Or at least a simulacrum of that lover. Just as I am bound to the mind of the forest. Already I can feel my individual thoughts becoming increasingly cloudy and intoxicated.

And I know this is how they will find us, with their laser rifles in hand. Unless our forest finds them first.

DEATH OF A DOME CITY

Boston

Safe in the aseptic hold
of our geodesic dome,
where the air is circulated
constantly and passes
through hundreds of filters
to assure its purity,
we remain protected
from the implacable horror
of the Mutant Rain Forest.

Yet across the horizon
we see the forest advance
from the south like a dense
and mottled green army.
Creatures from that world
roam beyond it by night.
The squatters that once
surrounded our city
have fled to the north,
the makeshift dwellings
and happenstance streets
of their shantytown
now deserted of life.

Sealed in the womb
of our transparent dome,
fueled by renewable energy,
where all matter is recycled,
where molecular structures
are formed and reformed

to satisfy our every need,
we remain self-sufficient.
We live a life of relaxation,
of plenty and pleasure,
experiencing all manner
of virtual entertainments
that our ancestors could
never have envisioned.

Yet the forest continues
to advance without respite.
We watch the flames
from our laser cannons
blacken the encroaching
walls of noxious vegetation.
We see a rain of defoliants
stream from defensive towers,
endlessly spraying the forest.

Like some sentient being
the forest responds with
massive storms of pollen,
dead leaves, shreds of bark,
clogging the mechanisms
of our devices and burying
them beneath mounds
of particulate debris,
more fertile ground for
its growth to colonize.

Trapped in the prison
of our impregnable dome
where daylight shrinks

as huge lianas with
suckered pods climb
the transparent walls,
soon we no longer see
the sun or the heavens.
The streetlights burn
through day and night.
And a wondrous and
compelling fragrance
fills the air we breathe.

THE MUTANT FORESTS OF MARS
Frazier

In the shuttered enclaves of the overrun Americas
Where green carries a stigma of the purely untouchable
They whisper of the Frog Spirit's moonfaced countenance

Beside the snow-crusted Scandinavian valley roads
Where only the most agile or artful dare to tread
Its wolf blood and Fenrir lines that chill the bone

Across the silvery dusts of the Sea of Tranquility
Where the horizon is marred by compressor towers
The lunar faithful give thanks for their sterile isolation

Every culture every ecosystem every tongue
Touched by the extensive reach of mutation
Has a blasphemous name for this agent of change

But on the terraformed red dirt plains of Mars
Historical references are lost on the colonists
They snort and sneer at such literate romanticism

They consider it more a bioagent of inevitability
Born from rain forests bred in wild profusion
It stowed away on every sunship and shuttle

From behind the pearly sheen of energy shields
The new Martians call it simply the "god trait"
Deepest sleeper in our evolving genomics

West of the Olympus Mons volcanic cone
Water ices reacted with lava flows to create
The cobwebbed networks of *Amazonis Planitia*

The newly populated flats and crags teem with
Barely recognizable variants on an Earthly scourge
Semi-sentient kudzu with meristem brain bulbs

And the vast reiterations of the gargantua trees
Cast long shadows over the lairs of red duendes
Neon toucans ghost lemurs necrophida moths

Here the resilient inhabitants the Schiaparellites
Push back these aggressive advances of untrue biota
And too fight the psychoactive ravages of pavonine

They consult the first mystics and forest explorers
They consult the Book of Genna for any slight clue
To the origins and evolutions of what they become

With a stoic ear attuned to the great green voice
They await the corruption's disarmingly hot embrace
And their impending ascension toward the unknown

Toward the unholy annexation of all human forms

Robert Frazier lives on Nantucket Island, once known as the center of the American whaling industry, with his wife, Karol Lindquist, a nationally recognized basket maker. He works as the curator of exhibitions for the Artists Association of Nantucket, and has oil paintings in galleries in New York State, Cape Cod, and on the island (visit www.oldspoutergallery.com). He has attended the Clarion Writers Workshop, Sycamore Hill Writer's Workshop, and the Franklinia Workshop. Frazier is the author of nine books of poetry, and a three-time winner of the Rhysling Award, as well as an *Asimov's* Reader Award for poetry. He was on the 1991 final ballot for a Nebula Award for fiction (collaborating with Lucius Shepard). Over 100 poems have appeared in *Asimov's SF,* as well as in *The Twilight Zone Magazine, F&SF, Omni,* and other anthologies and publications. His books include *Perception Barriers, The Daily Chernobyl,* and *Phantom Navigation.* He received the Grandmaster Award of the Science Fiction Poetry Association in 2005.

Bruce Boston lives in Ocala, Florida, once known as the City of Trees, with his wife, writer-artist Marge Simon, and the ghosts of two cats. He is the author of more than fifty books and chapbooks, including the dystopian sf novel *The Guardener's Tale* and the psychedelic coming-of-age noel *Stained Glass Rain.* His work has appeared in hundreds of publications, including *Asimov's SF Magazine, Analog, Amazing Stories, Weird Tales, Strange Horizons, Realms of Fantasy, Daily Science Fiction, Year's Best Fantasy and Horror,* and *The Nebula Awards Showcase.* One of the leading genre poets for more than thirty years, Boston has won the Bram Stoker Award for Poetry Collection, the *Asimov's* Readers Award for Poetry, and the

Rhysling Award for Speculative Poetry, each a record number of times. He has also received a Pushcart Prize for Fiction and the first Grandmaster Award of the Science Fiction Poetry Association. Currently, in addition to his writing, he edits speculative poetry for *The Pedestal Magazine*. www.bruceboston.com.

Luke Spooner currently lives and works in the South of England. Having graduated from the University of Portsmouth with a first-class degree he is now a fulltime illustrator working under two aliases: "Carrion House" for his darker work and "Hoodwink House" for his work aimed at a younger audience. He believes that the job of putting someone else's words into a visual form, to accompany and support their text, is a massive responsibility as well as being something he truly treasures.

The end? Not quite...

Have you read **Bruce Boston's** *Brief Encounters with My Third Eye* Over one hundred of Boston's best short poems (under fifty lines) from more than forty years of publishing, including fifteen award-winning poems.

If you enjoyed this book, we're certain you'll also like the following Crystal Lake titles:

Gutted: Beautiful Horror Stories An anthology of dark fiction that explores the beauty at the very heart of darkness. Featuring horror's most celebrated voices: Clive Barker, Neil Gaiman, Ramsey Campbell, Paul Tremblay, John F.D. Taff, Lisa Mannetti, Damien Angelica Walters, Josh Malerman, Christopher Coake, Mercedes M. Yardley, Brian Kirk, Stephanie M. Wytovich, Amanda Gowin, Richard Thomas, Maria Alexander, and Kevin Lucia.

Tribulations **by Richard Th**omas In the third short story collection by Richard Thomas, *Tribulations*, these stories cover a wide range of dark fiction—from fantasy, science fiction and horror, to magical realism, neo-noir, and transgressive fiction. The common thread that weaves these tragic tales together is suffering and sorrow, and the ways we emerge from such heartbreak stronger, more appreciative of what we have left—a spark of hope enough to guide us though the valley of death.

The Dark at the End of the Tunnel **by Taylor Grant** Offered for the first time in a collected format, this selection features ten gripping and darkly imaginative stories by Taylor Grant, a Bram Stoker Award ® nominated author and rising star in the suspense and horror genres. Grant exposes the terrors that hide beneath the surface of our ordinary world, behind people's masks of normalcy, and lurking in the shadows at the farthest reaches of the universe.

The Outsiders Lovecraftian shared-world anthology. They'll do anything to protect their way of life. Anything. Welcome to Priory, a small gated community in the UK, where the only thing worse than an ancient monster is the group worshipping it. Is that which slithers below true evil, or does evil reside in the people of Priory? Includes stories by Stephen Bacon, James Everington, Rosanne Rabinowitz, V.H. Leslie, and Gary Fry.

***Eden Underground* horror poetry by Alessandro Manzetti** Another snake, another tree, another Eve. A surreal journey into obsessions and aberrations of the modern world and the darker side, which often takes control of the situation. Winner of the 2014 Bram Stoker Award for Superior Achievement in Poetry.

If you ever thought of becoming an author, we recommend these non-fiction titles:

Horror 101: The Way Forward A comprehensive overview of the Horror fiction genre and career opportunities available to established and aspiring authors, including Jack Ketchum, Graham Masterton, Edward Lee, Lisa Morton, Ellen Datlow, Ramsey Campbell, and many more.

Horror 201: The Silver Scream Vol.1 and Vol.2 A must read for anyone interested in the horror film industry.

Includes interviews and essays by Wes Craven, John Carpenter, George A. Romero, Mick Garris, and dozens more. Now available in a special paperback edition.

***Modern Mythmakers: 35 interviews with Horror and Science Fiction Writers and Filmmakers* by Michael McCarty** Ever wanted to hang out with legends like Ray Bradbury, Richard Matheson, and Dean Koontz? Modern Mythmakers is your chance to hear fun anecdotes and career advice from authors and filmmakers like Forrest J. Ackerman, Ray Bradbury, Ramsey Campbell, John Carpenter, Dan Curtis, Elvira, Neil Gaiman, Mick Garris, Laurell K. Hamilton, Jack Ketchum, Dean Koontz, Graham Masterton, Richard Matheson, John Russo, William F. Nolan, John Saul, Peter Straub, and many more.

Writers On Writing: An Author's Guide Your favorite authors share their secrets in the ultimate guide to becoming and being and author. Writers On Writing is an eBook series with original 'On Writing' essays by writing professionals.

Or check out other Crystal Lake Publishing books
for Tales from The Darkest Depths.

Hi, readers. It makes our day to know you reached the end of our book. Thank you so much. This is why we do what we do every single day.

Whether you found the book good or great, we'd love to hear what you thought. Please take a moment to leave a review on Amazon, Goodreads, or anywhere else readers visit. Reviews go a long way to helping a book sell, and will help us to continue publishing quality books.

Thank you again for taking the time to journey with Crystal Lake Publishing. We are also on...

Website:
www.crystallakepub.com
(be sure to sign up for our newsletter and receive two free eBooks)

Books:
http://www.crystallakepub.com/books.php

Twitter:
https://twitter.com/crystallakepub

Facebook:
https://www.facebook.com/Crystallakepublishing/

Pinterest:
https://za.pinterest.com/crystallakepub/

Instagram:
https://www.instagram.com/crystal_lake_publishing/

Patreon:
https://www.patreon.com/CLP

We'd love to hear from you. Or check out other Crystal Lake Publishing books (www.crystallakepub.com/books) for your Dark Fiction, Horror, Suspense, and Thriller needs.

With unmatched success since 2012, Crystal Lake Publishing has quickly become one of the world's leading indie publishers of Mystery, Thriller, and Suspense books with a Dark Fiction edge.

Crystal Lake Publishing puts integrity, honor and respect at the forefront of our operations. We strive for each book and outreach program that's launched to not only entertain and touch or comment on issues that affect our readers, but also to strengthen and support the Dark Fiction field and its authors.

Not only do we publish authors who are legends in the field and as hardworking as us, but we look for men and women who care about their readers and fellow human beings. We only publish the very best Dark Fiction, and look forward to launching many new careers.
We strive to know each and every one of our readers, while building personal relationships with our authors, reviewers, bloggers, pod-casters, bookstores and libraries.

Crystal Lake Publishing is and will always be a beacon of what passion and dedication, combined with overwhelming teamwork and respect, can accomplish: Unique fiction you can't find anywhere else.

We do not just publish books, we present you worlds within your world, doors within your mind, from talented authors who sacrifice so much for a moment of your time.

This is what we believe in. What we stand for. This will be our legacy.

Welcome to Crystal Lake Publishing.

We hope you enjoyed this title. If so, we'd be grateful if you could leave a review on your blog or any of the other websites and outlets open to book reviews. Reviews are like gold to writers and publishers, since word-of-mouth is and will always be the best way to market a great book. And remember to keep an eye out for more of our books.

THANK YOU FOR PURCHASING THIS BOOK